For such a confirmed bachelor and des-
piser of women, Bradley Dexter was surprisingly fond of their company—but of
course it was the 'double standard',
Robyn thought furiously; he sneered at
them and used them—but woe betide any
woman who behaved the same way! Then
fate dropped her into just the right situation to give him a well-deserved lesson.
Except that fate then proceeded to play
tricks on Robyn herself!

CONFIRMED BACHELOR

BY

ROBERTA LEIGH

MILLS & BOON LIMITED
15–16 BROOK'S MEWS
LONDON W1A 1DR

First published 1981
Australian copyright 1981
Philippine copyright 1981
This edition 1981

© Roberta Leigh 1981

ISBN 0 263 73540 0

Set in Monophoto Baskerville 10 on 11 pt.

Made and printed in Great Britain by Richard Clay (The Chaucer Press) Ltd, Bungay, Suffolk

CHAPTER ONE

THE moment Robyn Barrett walked into her boss's office and saw his face, she knew something was wrong.

'Brad Dexter can't finish his book for us in time,' Morton Phillips announced. 'The earliest he can do it is by Christmas—and by then it will be too late.'

'It will still sell half a million,' Robyn placated.

'If we bring it out to coincide with the television series he's doing—which was the sole reason we wanted him to finish the book so quickly—we'd sell two million.'

There was nothing Robyn could say to this, for everything her employer said was right. Bradley Dexter was Morton Publications' best-selling author and also—in her opinion—one of its most obnoxious. Not that she had ever met him, for on the one occasion when he had come to the office she had been away ill. Every book he wrote became a best-seller around the world, and every book was on the same theme: anti-women—except as playthings; anti-marriage; anti-commitment of any kind. All the young men Robyn knew professed to dislike his views, yet nearly all of them bought his books, quoted his sarcastic quips and assiduously watched the television series which were always made from each of his books.

But six months ago he had devised a concept solely for the TV screen; called *Safety in Numbers*, it was a light-hearted romp through history showing how man had successfully fought his way out of the marriage trap. Hearing about it, Morton Phillips had immediately urged him to turn it into a book, which he was now in the process of doing.

'Why can't Mr Dexter finish it as promised?' Robyn

asked. 'The last time he was late on delivery, it was because he'd skipped off to Bali to escape from Miss World.'

'There's no woman involved this time,' her employer said. 'It's a man.'

'*What?*'

'No, no, not that! Martin—his secretary—has just had a water-skiing accident and won't be able to type for at least two months.'

'Why can't he get another secretary?'

'Because he won't work with someone he doesn't know, and he doesn't give a damn whether the book comes out or not. He's made himself a millionaire five times over with what he's already written, and he doesn't care if he never writes anything again.'

'Some writer,' Robyn said derisively. 'He's just a money-making machine.'

'Don't knock our bread and butter!'

'*My* bread and butter,' Robyn grinned. 'Your jam!'

Morton Phillips chuckled. Robyn had worked for him for two years and, despite her youth, was the best secretary he had ever had. When he had first engaged her, with an excellent recommendation from her previous employer, he had found it hard to credit that such a glamorous-looking girl could have brains to equal her beauty. But she had. And wit and charm too. So much, that he had found himself breaking his cardinal rule not to have an affair with anyone working for him, and had done all he could to entice her into his bed. But to no avail. Robyn, he had quickly discovered, had a will of iron beneath her soft exterior. Her golden-blonde hair, limpid grey eyes and voluptuous figure—always seen to advantage in the latest *Vogue* fashions—was an old-fashioned girl who yearned for a cottage in the country, a loving husband and a brood of children.

The fact that she had not found what she was looking for was no one's fault but her own; for she was exceptionally choosy, and knew exactly what she wanted, and had no intention of compromising. But why should she? A girl with her looks and brains could get any man she liked. With an effort he brought his mind away from the delicate curve of her mouth to the more pressing problem of Bradley Dexter's refusal to complete the book until his secretary was able to work for him again.

'Damn ridiculous!' he exploded. 'I've already booked the advertising, committed the printers, and landed myself with a hell of a lot of expense. Brad's got to complete this book in time—Martin's not the only secretary in the world, though you'd think he was, from the way Brad goes on about him.'

'How long has he been working for Mr Dexter?' Robyn asked curiously.

'Since he began writing, which was about ten years ago.'

'I'm surprised he doesn't have a female secretary—knowing how much he loves our sex.'

'He only loves them if he knows he can leave them,' Morton Phillips said dryly. 'Which is why he feels safer with Martin.'

'Do you want me to ring up our advertising agency and cancel the adverts we've booked for Mr Dexter?'

'No, don't do anything yet. I'm not giving in to Brad's decision without putting up a fight. The whole thing's nonsensical. There must be any number of male secretaries he can get. I'm going to call him again and see if I can twist his arm.'

He reached for the telephone, a frown marring his thin, faintly lined face. Tall, slim, and a well-groomed forty-five, Morton Phillips was the epitome of the urbane publisher. Robyn watched him for a moment, then went out, thinking dark thoughts about Bradley Dexter's high-handed behaviour. He knew very well that his publisher had expended a great deal of money to promote this forthcoming book, and from what she remembered Morton telling her, it now needed no more than five or six weeks' work on it to complete it. It was typical Dexter arrogance to refuse to do so until his secretary was fit again.

Come to think of it, she was not sure she even believed the excuse. It was more likely that Bradley Dexter was caught up in another one of his temporary but highly publicised interludes with yet another of the world's beauties. Names and faces flashed into her mind and flashed out of it as quickly as they did his life. He really was the world's worst playboy—or best—depending on your viewpoint. And to make matters worse, he used each affair as grist to his mill, basing his books on his experiences.

An office junior came in with a percolator of freshly brewed coffee and set it on Robyn's desk. She sniffed the aroma appreciatively, then poured a cup to take in to her employer After a conversation with Mr Dexter he would be in need of it! With her usual silent efficiency she glided into his office and placed the cup at his elbow. His ear was glued to the receiver, and the frown on his face had intensified, telling her that his conversation with his best, and most difficult, author was, as usual, onerous.

'Have your coffee,' she mouthed, and lightly tapped his arm.

He looked up. 'Thanks, Robyn.' Picking up the cup, he gave his attention back to his call. 'What did you say?' he said into the receiver. 'No, I'm not talking to someone else at the same time as I'm talking to you. I was merely thanking my secretary for bringing me some coffee. Although at the moment I'd prefer a stiff whisky.'

He paused and held the receiver away from his ear so that Robyn could hear the staccato voice coming through it. She could not make out what was being said, though it seemed to amuse her boss, who was half-smiling.

'I can assure you that Robyn's just as good as Martin,' Morton Phillips stated. 'He's not the only competent secretary, you know. Why you should think you can't find anyone to take his place for a couple of months beats me. If you——'

He stopped as the staccato voice interrupted him, and Robyn, deciding the conversation was going to go on for some time, went to the door. Her hand was on the knob when she heard her boss give a startled exclamation.

'But that's impossible! How can I . . . Dammit! Can't you get someone down there? Yes, I know I said Robyn was the best, but . . .' With an anguished look in her direction, Morton Phillips motioned her to stay.

Robyn shook her head, mouthing that she had no intention whatever of becoming Mr Dexter's secretary for two minutes, let alone two months, but her employer deliberately closed his eyes as he went on speaking.

'Well, if that's the way you feel, Brad, I don't have any choice. How long do you think it will be for? Very well, but no more than six weeks, and on the firm understanding that the book is finished in that time.' He put the phone down quickly, before Bradley Dexter changed his mind, then opened his eyes and looked at his secretary. 'I had no choice,' he said weakly. 'You know how much this book means to us.'

'So you're throwing me to the wolf, are you?' Robyn said crossly. 'Don't you have any sense of guilt?'

'Only to my bank manager!' Brown eyes surveyed her. 'Be a pet and do it, Robyn. I *would* feel guilty if I didn't know you better, but you're more than able to take care of yourself—otherwise you wouldn't still be such an innocent!'

'How right you are,' she said crisply. 'Bradley Dexter won't get any change from me! He's everything I despise.'

'For God's sake don't tell him until the book's finished!

I'm depending on you to see he gets it done.'

'Don't worry about *that*. I'll make sure his nose is kept to the grindstone!'

'See that he keeps his hands there too! Those Mediterranean nights can be dangerous.'

'Even to a girl armoured in innocence?' Robyn chided, then asked curiously: 'I'm surprised he wanted me to work for him. I thought he kept women out of his professional life.'

'You're the exception that proves the rule,' her employer replied. 'I guess it's because he's heard me speak of you before. You wrote to him a few months ago suggesting some amendments, and he called and said he thought you were right, and that you had a good brain.'

'Good enough not to stand any nonsense from him,' she retorted.

'And tactful enough not to let him know what you think of him, I hope?'

'Of course,' Robyn said sweetly. 'I have the interests of the company at heart. How soon do you want me to go?'

'Will the end of the week suit you? Take the next two days off to buy yourself some summery clothes, and charge the bills to me. Then try to get yourself on a plane on Friday.'

'I suppose I do have to go?' said Robyn, suddenly getting cold feet at the thought of having to work for a modern-day Casanova.

'For the good of the company,' Morton Phillips reminded her. 'You said it yourself.'

Sighing, Robyn left the room, in search of a much-needed cup of coffee for herself.

It was not until Friday afternoon, comfortably ensconced in a first-class seat on her way to Nice, a case full of new clothes in the hold, which she rightfully saw as sugar on the bitter pill she was forced to swallow for the next six weeks, that Robyn began to feel deeply apprehensive at what lay ahead of her. Although she had no fear of falling prey to Bradley Dexter's undoubted charms—from the interviews she had seen him give on television she was wise enough not to underrate them—she knew that her own appearance would make him determined to add her to his collection of female scalps.

In fact, the more obvious she made her dislike of him, the more determined he might be to seduce her. That left her with two options. Either to be so clinging and sweet that she would irritate him to distraction—in which case he might send her packing and not finish the book—or to be so hardboiled that she would scare him off. As the plane winged its way over the lush green countryside of France, and then the snowy caps of the Alps, she was no nearer deciding which course of action to take, and was still grappling with the problem when the plane landed at Nice airport.

Although she knew no one was going to meet her, she could not help experiencing a pang of loneliness as she crossed the terminal hall to wait for her luggage. Morton Phillips had told her to take a taxi to Bradley Dexter's villa, which was some ten miles from the airport on Cap d'Antibes.

The taxi driver seemed to know the address quite well, for he gave her a decided leer as he gallantly opened the door for her. Robyn, used to such looks, was also immune to them, and she settled back in her seat and stared with interest at the passing scene. Within minutes of leaving the airport they were on the coast road, and her spirits revived at sight of the nodding palms and scintillating blue sea, several shades deeper than the clear sky.

If only she were coming here to work for a man she could respect rather than despise. But at least she would be in glamorous surroundings, for the pictures she had seen of Mr Dexter's villa showed it to be one of the loveliest on the coast. She wondered which one of his many girl-friends would be in residence, having no illusion that pressure of work would stop him from pursuing his favourite sport. Her soft mouth tightened, and she forcibly reminded herself that it was not her business to pass judgment on the way a person led their life, providing they did not harm anyone except themselves. Certainly the women in Bradley Dexter's life all seemed to know the score, and were not to be pitied when he left them high and dry. Yet everything he represented was anathema to her, and she mused on the life she wanted for herself— which was totally different from that of this arrogant, best-selling author.

Born late in life to doting parents who had long given up hope of a child, she had been seen as a gift from God, and the fact that she had been beautiful to look at and docile by nature had confirmed them in this belief. Her childhood and teenage had been idyllic: a beautiful Queen Anne house in a small Wiltshire village, which she had only left to attend a private school in a nearby town. Although clever enough to go to university, she had not felt sufficient compulsion towards any particular career, and had finally decided on a secretarial one.

It was not until she was in her first job in London that Robyn realised what a handicap her looks were. She had always taken her appearance for granted—as had all the friends with whom she had grown up. But the new ones she made left her in no doubt that silver-blonde hair— thick and with a natural soft wave—atop a tall, slender body, and a face classical in its symmetry of feature, could get her almost any man she wanted. The trouble was, she never met anyone she *did* want—except as a friend— which few men found satisfying.

Her parents, who were longing for her to settle down and give them grandchildren, could not understand why, from her countless horde of admirers, she could not choose one, and their matchmaking instincts made weekends at home somewhat tiresome. Guilt sometimes made Robyn wonder if she should accept the next suitable proposal that came along. After all, what was she waiting for? A romantic knight in shining armour to sweep her off her feet?

The answer was yes, for she was an incurable romantic, with old-fashioned ideas of morality, despite living in an age when romance was unfashionable. Her girl friends fell in and out of bed with little thought; accepting it as a way of saying thank you for a nice evening, in the same way that their mothers had bestowed a kiss, a generation before them. They teased Robyn for her old-fashioned stance, but had long since given up trying to bring her round to their way of thinking. Sex without love was a concept she had been brought up to abhor, and she saw no reason to change her mind, nor her belief in the sanctity of marriage.

The taxi swung sharply to the right and Robyn saw they had veered away from the coast and were driving along a wide promontory that jutted out into the sea. This was Cap d'Antibes, site of some of the most beautiful villas on the coast, and now the home of many wealthy Arabs who, together with Greek tycoons, spent their summers here. And Bradley Dexter too, of course. This was his base, between peripatetic jaunts around the world in search of fun, or running away from commitments. But for the next weeks he would be staying put—she would see to that—until he had finished the book for her firm.

Another right turn brought them to a cypress-lined road. On one side she glimpsed parkland and the tall graceful columns of a house—the Niarchos villa, her taxi driver informed her—and on the other a high stone wall which wound for hundreds of yards before giving way to massive iron gates. It was here that the car stopped and the driver jumped out and spoke into the little grid inset into one of the stone pillars. The gates swung open and the driver jumped behind the wheel and drove smartly through them, before they swung shut again.

For a quarter of a mile they wended their way along an imposing driveway, until they finally rounded a bend and saw the villa before them.

Villa? Robyn thought in astonishment. It was more like a miniature palace. Long and low, except for a tall tower at one end, its walls were marble-clad, giving the impression of a French Taj Mahal. A flight of shallow steps led up to an imposing front door, banked on either side by purple bougainvillaea. A dozen cars, American, French and English, were parked in the circular forecourt, in the centre of which a huge fountain sprayed cool water over a profusion of waterlilies and goldfish.

There was no one in sight, but as Robyn stepped out of the taxi she heard the faint sound of music coming from the far side of the house, and guessed that here lay the pool. The taxi driver carried her cases up to the front door and eyed her appreciatively as she paid him, then careered away down the drive, grinning all over his face. He probably thinks I'm another one of Mr Dexter's birds, she thought irritably, and rang the doorbell.

There was no answer and she waited with growing impatience. A second firm pressure on the bell still brought no reply, and she tentatively turned the handle. To her surprise the door swung open, and she entered a vast, circular hall. Everything was marble here too, white as the outside walls, but with a fine vein of gold and pink which matched the Persian silk rugs scattered on the floor. A marble staircase with wrought iron railings wound gracefully up to the first floor—where the bedrooms presumably were, though it was the downstairs rooms which held her attention.

A huge living room lay directly in front of her, its southern facing wall completely glass. It was filled with countless suede-covered armchairs and leather chesterfields, all in pale colours, which made them look like fat fruit-drops on the shiny marble floor. Glass and gold tables were dotted between them, and there were flowers everywhere, their colours vying with the startlingly modern paintings placed strategically around the walls. Robyn shuddered as she looked at them. She liked modern art, but these seemed to have come from another galaxy. Her opinion of Mr Dexter sank even lower.

It was only as she stepped into the room that she saw that at the far end, on her left, lay a dining area, furnished with a beautiful teak table and chairs—capacity for twenty people at least. To the right of her lay a similar area, but two steps down in level, and here were booklined walls and a cinema screen. Resolutely she moved across the room, her body supple in a grey silk suit that was almost the same colour as her eyes. It was an unusual colour for a blonde to wear, and no one other than Robyn would have thought of it. But it gave her hair a silvery quality which increased the innocent look of a small, full mouth and faintly tiptilted nose.

As she neared the glass wall she had a better view of the wide terrace that ran the entire length of the house. It was some fifteen feet in depth and was scattered with whitewood furniture: tables and chaises-longues with gaily coloured parasols that matched the half dozen hammocks which stood empty.

Curiously she advanced further, but not until she actually walked on to the terrace did she glimpse the next level of land and see, some eight feet below, a kidney-shaped swimming pool, Olympic in size and tiled completely with green and blue mosaic.

Robyn gasped and recoiled. Not at the pool, nor the bright mattresses ranged around it; not at the loud music blaring from hidden speakers, nor at the pagoda-shaped bar where a Vietnamese butler was busily pouring drinks, but at the dozen or so men and girls boisterously playing in the pool—topless every one of them—and some of them bottomless too.

Heavens! she thought. This is even worse than I expected. Dismay and anger kept her rooted to the spot. How dared Morton Phillips send her here? Didn't he know what was going on? And what sort of woman did Bradley Dexter take her for? She searched among the crowd for him, and almost instantly found him. He was not one of the laughing men in the water, as she had assumed, but a motionless, almost sardonic-looking figure sitting on the edge of the pool, near the diving board. Even from a distance she saw that his pictures failed to do him justice. He was even better looking than they depicted. Because he was sitting down it was hard to tell his height, but he was well over six foot, with the build of an athlete. He was darker than she had expected: his skin tanned mahogany, and his hair blue-black. Aware that her heart was thumping uncomfortably fast, Robyn drew a deep breath and walked down the steps towards him.

Nobody in the pool took any notice of her, too intent on their own pleasures. Only the man at the far end watched her approach and, as she drew nearer, his cool appraisal raked her from head to toe. She began to tremble. Was it with temper or fear? She was no longer sure. She stopped a few feet away from him and had her first clear glimpse of his face. Ah yes, this was Bradley Dexter all right. She'd know those hazel eyes anywhere, and that mocking, wide mouth. But his nose seemed stronger and more dominant than it looked on television, and his chin more pugnacious too, rising above a thick, strong throat around which hung a gold medallion. Typical, she thought.

'Better late than never, beautiful,' he said indolently, leaning back on an elbow to appraise her yet again. 'Take off your clothes and jump in.'

'*What?*'

'There's no need to be shy.' His accent was faintly

American and she remembered that his mother had been one. 'Divest yourself, honey, and take the plunge.'

'Do you have any soap?' she asked sweetly.

'Soap?'

'For me to wash with. That's the only time I jump naked into the water!'

For an instant he stared at her, then he gave a slow smile that showed gleaming white teeth.

All the better to eat you with, she thought, and knew that next to him, the wolf was but a lamb.

'Okay, you've made your point,' he drawled, 'but if you don't want to join us, why are you here?'

'Because Mr Phillips sent me.'

'Mr who?'

'Mr Morton Phillips—your publisher. I'm his secretary, Robyn Barrett.'

Finely curved dark eyebrows drew together, and Robyn wondered if Bradley Dexter suffered from amnesia. Surely he hadn't forgotten she was coming here?

'I don't believe it,' he said finally. 'Morton wouldn't do this to me. He said he was sending a man.'

'He said he was sending you his secretary. And that's me.'

'Robyn!' Her name was said softly, though the expression on his face was hard. 'My God, Morton did it deliberately! He knows damn well I won't employ a woman.'

'Mr Phillips sent me because you asked him,' Robyn said succinctly. 'Because you practically *ordered* him to do it. He did *not* offer, Mr Dexter. I know,' she added, 'because I was in the room and heard you on the telephone.'

'It was a mistake,' Bradley Dexter said at once. 'I'm sorry you've had a wasted journey, Miss—er——'

'Barrett,' she said, and there and then made up her mind she was not going to give in to him. How dared he think he could order her and her boss around like this?

'You've engaged me for six weeks,' she said firmly, 'and

when I go back I intend taking your manuscript with me.'

'Is that so?' His eyes glittered, more green than grey. 'There's only one thing wrong with your statement, Miss Barrett. I'm *not*—definitely *not* working with a female. If I——'

A shrill peal of laughter cut off the rest of his words, and they both looked over to where a pretty young red-head, completely nude, was being tossed in the air by two husky young men, while everyone else in the pool was clapping and cheering.

Robyn tried to keep her face expressionless, but Bradley Dexter's next words told her she had not been successful.

'You can't stay,' he said when he could make himself heard again. 'You'd hate it here, and since I've no intention of altering my life style——'

'You wouldn't need to,' she interrupted. 'I'm not a prude, Mr Dexter.'

'Then undress and go into the pool!'

'It's too childish,' she said with disdain. 'I was playing those sort of games when I was sixteen. Besides, men bore me.'

'They do?'

'Very much so.' Robyn made herself sigh. 'That's one of the reasons I agreed to come here and work for you. Because you're so much a man after my own heart.'

'You'll have to explain that,' Bradley Dexter said, his face devoid of expression.

Robyn knew her test had come. Undecided what role to play, the part had now been thrust upon her. Trusting she would be able to live up to it, she said:

'Your first book has been my bible. It expressed everything I felt about the opposite sex. Your contempt for women is only equalled by *my* contempt for men. In that respect, Mr Dexter, we're soulmates. If I could write as well as you, I'd be writing the feminine equivalent of each one of your books!'

A spark of interest gleamed in the hazel eyes watching her. 'So you're a liberated female,' he commented. 'There's nothing unusual in that.'

'I'm not liberated in the usual way,' she stated, thrusting her hips forward aggressively. 'I don't need to prove my femininity by eschewing men. On the contrary, I use them when I need them, and drop them when I don't—the way you do with women.'

'Until Mr Right comes along for you,' he said, rising to his feet in one graceful movement, and looming over her, six foot three of perfectly co-ordinated muscle, only a small part of which was covered by tight, brief black trunks.

'There's no such thing as a Mr Right for me,' said Robyn and, stepping slightly back from him, gave him the same careful, appraising look he had given her. It took every ounce of her courage, and only her inner fury enabled her to do it. But it worked, for she saw surprise, quickly masked, flit across his face. 'You're a good-looking specimen, Mr Dexter, and when I decide to have a child, I wouldn't mind *you* as the father. But that won't be for at least five years yet, so there's no point our discussing it.'

This time he made no effort to hide his surprise. 'What makes you think I'd be willing to father your child, Miss Barrett?'

'Wouldn't you?' she asked, astonished. 'I'm far more intelligent than any of your girl-friends to date—and just as good to look at.'

'You love yourself, don't you?'

'No more than you do, Mr Dexter.'

He chuckled, and triumph coursed through her, though she was careful to hide it. This male chauvinist pig must believe her to be serious in everything she said. Nor must she lose her ability to surprise him. Only by doing so could she keep one jump ahead of him; and being one jump ahead was the only way she would be safe in this wolf's lair.

'If you could ask someone to show me to my room,' she went on, 'I'd like to change.'

'Would you object to being in the next room to mine?'

'I'm quite willing to share yours, provided you don't snore.'

He blinked. 'Are you serious?'

'Why shouldn't I be? You've got a fantastic body, Mr Dexter, and I think you'd be quite a good lover.'

'You're very experienced, I suppose?'

'Not as experienced as you,' she replied. 'But I've been more selective.'

'I happen to be very selective, Miss Barrett. And you don't happen to be my type.'

'Gone off blondes, have we?' she asked pertly.

'For the moment,' he said sourly, and flicked his fingers in the direction of the bar. The Vietnamese came forward and Bradley Dexter asked him to show his guest to her room.

As Robyn walked away from the pool, Bradley Dexter dived in to join the screaming occupants, and his shout of laughter rang in her ears as she walked into the house.

It was only when she was alone in her bedroom that her nerves got the better of her and, shaking like a leaf, she sank down in an easy chair by the window. Slowly she began to relax and take in her surroundings. She had been given a beautiful room, and she was surprised to see that its decor was quite unlike the modern rooms downstairs. It was furnished with a hand-painted French bed and dressing table, with matching bedside tables, and fitted cupboards whose sliding doors were skilfully decorated to blend in with the period. The walls were draped in pale blue silk, and sapphire blue carpet—the thickest she had seen—lay underfoot.

If this was the room Mr Dexter had planned for a male secretary, he must have been expecting a very odd one, she thought, and wondered curiously what his own secretary was like. A eunuch, perhaps, who would give him no competition with the ladies. She giggled as she remembered his expression when she had suggested sharing his room. She had taken a calculated risk, and, had she lost it, would have had to hotfoot it back to London. Luckily the risk had paid off, and her boldness had annoyed rather than encouraged him. Pray to heaven it remained this way.

If Bradley Dexter liked to do the chasing, she would have to chase him so hard during the next six weeks that he'd be breathless from running away. But she must work out her tactics carefully, and decide exactly how best to keep him turned off.

Smiling at the thought, she stood up and started to unpack.

CHAPTER TWO

IT was lunch time when Robyn had put all her clothes away, and, wearing an emerald green sundress with a matching jacket, went downstairs to find out where she would be working. Kim, the butler, was crossing the hall as she reached it, and she gave him a tentative smile.

'Where does Mr Dexter do his writing?' she asked.

'In his private suite,' the Vietnamese replied.

Robyn swallowed. 'Not in his study?' she questioned, pointing to the far end of the living room.

'That only for visitors and newspapers photographers. Mr Dexter does serious work in own room.'

I don't doubt it, Robyn thought.

'Come,' the man said. 'I show you.' She hesitated, and a slight smile passed over his impassive features. 'Mr Dexter still by pool,' he assured her, and glided ahead of her up the stairs.

Nervously Robyn followed him back to the first floor, passed her own room and into the turret at the far end of the corridor. It was like entering another world: a fairytale one of Mogul splendour, with Kashmir rugs on the floor, jewel-like miniatures on the walls, and ivory inlaid furniture.

'Mr Dexter very fond of Eastern decor,' Kim said.

'Then why is the downstairs so modern?' she asked.

'He like modern too. He say variety is——'

'The spice of life,' she finished, and decided that if the author was going to be as predictable in everything, it wouldn't be too difficult to fool him.

Bradley Dexter's bedroom was at the top of the turret and had a breathtaking view of La Garoupe lighthouse on one side, and the bay of Juan on the other, while in between, villas in white, pink and beige stucco lay tucked

among the palms and cypresses, coy as young girls from
prying eyes. His bedroom was as glamorous as that of a
potentate, with an eight-foot circular bed set below a
mirrored ceiling, and skilfully hidden lights controlled
from a panel inset into the gold headboard.

'I can't see a typewriter,' Robyn commented.

'Study is below.' Kim opened a narrow door and disclosed a delicate spiral staircase.

Following him down, Robyn found herself in a room
as efficient as that of a director at space headquarters on
Cape Canaveral. The newest in word processors stood
alongside a gleaming steel dictating machine. Next to this
were three telephones, and a bank of clocks showing the
different times in London, New York, Tokyo and
Sydney—countries where Mr Dexter's books sold in their
millions.

'How efficient,' she murmured. 'But unfortunately I
don't know how to use a word processor.'

Kim opened a cupboard and she saw the latest IBM
electric typewriter. It made her feel better just to look at
it, and she asked him to put it on the desk. Unable to
hide his surprise, he did as he was ordered.

'I really *am* Mr Dexter's temporary secretary,' she
stated. 'Did you think I was pretending?'

'Ladies do,' he shrugged. 'Many come here, and all
have different stories. But they all here for one thing.'

'I don't doubt it,' Robyn said primly. 'How long have
you worked for Mr Dexter?'

'Ten years—but no woman stay longer than two, three
months.'

'Ten years!' Robyn exclaimed, more interested in this
man than his employer's love life. 'But you look so young.'

'I'm thirty-four,' he said. 'Same age as Mr Dexter. He
found me in refugee camp and get me and wife out. I
work for him ever since.'

'Wouldn't you like to do something else?'

Kim shook his head. 'Mr Dexter offer me chance to study, but I happy to stay with him. My wife wish stay here too,' he added. 'We travel all places with him. Is excellent life.'

Robyn made a mental note not to give herself away to this boyish-looking man whose first loyalty was undoubtedly to the employer he worshipped.

'I'll come back here to do some work when I've had lunch,' she announced. 'Perhaps Mr Dexter will give me something to be getting on with?'

'Mr Dexter never work when he have guests,' Kim informed her, his nut-brown features respectful but firm. 'You take lunch by pool with other guests?'

'No,' she said. 'I'd prefer to be alone. I'll eat on the terrace, if I may.'

Even though she did, she could still hear the noise from the poolside below her: laughter interspersed with the popping of champagne corks, and the occasional splash as someone dived into the pool to cool off. By half past two, silence reigned, and curiosity made her cross the flagstones and peer down.

Kim and another young man had cleared away all the food, and somnolent figures lay supine on the mattresses; some were occupied singly and some with couples. Quickly Robyn scanned the figures for sight of her temporary boss. He lay sprawled on a hammock, a girl either side of him, seemingly oblivious to the fact that one of them was stroking his hair and the other his feet. Resolutely, Robyn looked away.

She spent the afternoon in the study in the turret, carefully going through the half-finished manuscript which she had discovered in the top drawer of the desk. Like all Mr Dexter's work it was highly lucid, and witty; and even more anti-woman than anything he had yet written. Idly she wondered what made him so cynical about the female sex. She knew several men who did not wish to marry and enjoyed playing the field, but none had Mr Dexter's deep-seated dislike—almost loathing—of women. She was certain it came from more than a bachelor's fear of being caught. Perhaps he had had an unhappy love affair in his youth and had never recovered from it? He might even have been unhappily married. Whatever it was, it had turned him into the sort of person she despised.

She was still reading the manuscript when the sound of footsteps above her head made her realise that Bradley Dexter had returned to his bedroom. And not alone either, if the high-pitched giggle she heard was anything to go by. There was a faint slap of hand upon skin and another squeal which brought Robyn to her feet so sharply that her chair scraped across the floor.

A muttered oath told her it had been heard, and the door at the top of the spiral staircase opened. Bare feet padded downwards and Robyn's gaze rose to sinewy brown legs. Hastily she lowered her eyes.

'Who the hell's there?'

'It's only me, Mr Dexter.' Shaking with nerves, Robyn heard her voice come out as a thin thread of sound.

'Would only me mind getting the hell out of my private quarters and not coming back until asked!' he boomed.

Hurriedly Robyn obeyed, and only when she reached the safety of her own bedroom did her pulses cease their wild racing.

Fool, she chided herself. You should have stayed and brazened it out. Except that he might have been naked, a little voice reasoned, once again reminding her of the enormity of the task facing her. She reached for the telephone and, with shaking hands, put in a call to Morton Phillips.

His voice, warm and reassuring, did much to steady her, though it also made her unexpectedly tearful, as she blurted out everything that had happened since her arrival.

'I'd no idea I was letting you in for this kind of thing,' her employer muttered as she came to the end of her tale. 'But I'll be sunk if you come back now. To be honest, I got cold feet after you left for Nice this morning, and I tried to cancel all the advertising we'd placed for Bradley's book. But even though the agency will let me off the full cost, we'd still be down the drain for so much money that my entire profit for the year would be lost.'

'I know,' she mumbled. 'But I'm still not sure I can stick it here. He's impossible, Mr Phillips!'

'Then make yourself even more impossible. From what you've told me you haven't done badly so far! Look on it as a game, Robyn.'

By the time her call ended, Robyn had agreed to remain, though Morton Phillips promised that if she still felt unhappy in a week's time, she could return home.

For the next few hours Robyn remained in her room, afraid to venture downstairs in case she interrupted an orgy. But at eight o'clock, when she could no longer bear being cooped up, she tiptoed into the corridor and peered through one of the windows, relieved to see that all the cars had disappeared from the driveway. Only then did she go downstairs.

The villa seemed deserted, though soft lights glowed in the living room, and warmed the pink and gold marble walls of the hall. Remembering the shape of the villa, she walked through the dining room and found a door cunningly set into a flower-painted wall. It led to a tiled corridor and thence to a butler's pantry, where glass-fronted cupboards protected sets of exquisite china and silver. Another door opened into a large square kitchen, with stainless steel cabinets and primrose tiled walls and floor. A massive refrigerator and freezer hummed in one corner, and an equally massive electric oven stood alongside it. At the far end of the room an archway led through into a small dining area, surprisingly and charmingly furnished in French Provençal style, with wooden table and chairs and carved cabinets on the walls. It was here she found Kim and his wife, as plump as he was thin, as smiling as he was serious.

Kim jumped to his feet immediately he saw her.

'You ring bell,' he said quickly. 'We have dinner ready for you. Please go to dining room.'

'Must I?' Robyn pleaded. 'I'd much rather eat in here with you.'

The couple looked at one another, and Kim spoke softly to his wife in their own tongue. The woman looked startled, then glanced at Robyn warily. Robyn met her look and smiled, the first genuine one she had given since arriving here. Mrs Kim smiled back, then rose and bowed to a chair.

The next hour was Robyn's happiest at the villa. The Vietnamese couple were delightful to talk to, and though they were still somewhat reserved with her, Robyn was sure they would become friends before her stay was out. She had eaten the food Mrs Kim had prepared: a delicate blanquette de veau, and a tarte Tatin, but had begged to be allowed to sample their own Vietnamese food the following evening.

'Maybe you dine out tomorrow,' said Kim.

'Not if I can help it. I'm here to work.'

'Is not good work all time,' Mrs Kim said. 'Mr Dexter not let you stay alone each night. He have plenty friends you meet.'

'I'm not interested in having a social life here,' Robyn reiterated, and forbore to add that the quicker she got Bradley Dexter back to the grindstone, the quicker she would be able to leave.

She thought about this as she lay in bed that night, luxuriating in the softness of pure silk sheets—how extravagant could one get?—and glancing from time to time at the luminous hands of the little enamelled Lupin clock—another extravagance which Bradley Dexter extended to his guests. Really, the man must be worth a fortune, the way he spent his money!

Yet he was making a fortune too, if what Morton Phillips said was true. Could that be yet another reason why he was so cynical about women? Because he had fallen in love with one and discovered she only wanted him for his money? In which case, of course, the girl would have had to be blind as well as excessively stupid, for Mr Dexter—whether one liked his writing or not—was in every conceivable sense a superlative hunk of manhood.

Robyn was startled by her thoughts. She had never considered herself susceptible to the physical attributes of the male, believing that personality and character were far more important. Yet from the moment she had walked across the white flagstones bordering the pool, and become aware of mocking hazel eyes watching her, she had realised that her long-held belief was about to be shattered. It would be all too easy to fall for Bradley Dexter; and all too easy to end up with a broken heart.

Robyn's next conscious thought was of a dreadful thirst, and she sat up in bed and reached for her slippers. For a moment she was puzzled as to where she was. Then memory returned and, yawning, she pushed aside the silk coverlet and padded into the bathroom. The house was silent as a grave, though outside, leaves rustled as a nesting bird stirred, and a plaintive mewing sound signalled a cat or some other furry creature indigenous to the region.

Returning to the bedroom, a little more awake, she peeped through the open window. She had an excellent view of the pool. Although the floodlighting had been turned off, a few small lights glowed in the trees, and she noticed the dark shapes of two huge dogs padding around. She shivered. She must remember not to go out walking at night unless she wanted to be torn limb from limb. In the distance she heard the sound of a car and the squeal of brakes as a bend was taken too fast. Stupid driver, she thought and, as the sound came nearer, realised the car was approaching the house. She glanced at the clock. It was three-thirty. A car door slammed and she held her breath. No other sounds came and she moved back to the bed.

She was just pulling the coverlet over her when she heard someone singing cheerily as they passed her door. Indignantly she sat up, half afraid it would be opened. But it remained closed and the singing receded. Courage returning, Robyn went swiftly to the door and opened it. Peering out, she glimpsed Bradley Dexter's swaying figure at the far end of the corridor. Hastily she stepped back. What a time to come home! He certainly wouldn't be fit for work until midday. It really was too bad of him, when he had promised Morton Phillips faithfully that he would work flat out to get the book finished in time.

Fuming, Robyn returned to bed. She was too angry to sleep and lay there devising different ways of bringing Bradley Dexter to heel. Suddenly she chuckled. Of course! It was quite simple. She had already made him think she was Miss Logic personified, and now she would prove it to him. Reaching for the little clock, she set the alarm for seven-fifteen. That would just give her time to shower and dress before going in to awaken Mr Night-owl Dexter. How delighted he would be to see her!

As she stood outside the door of his bedroom at seven-thirty next morning, Robyn's courage almost failed her. Almost but not quite, and breathing deeply she pushed open the door and went in.

The room was in darkness, only a chink of light coming from between the closely drawn curtains. As her eyes grew accustomed to the gloom, she saw the single occupant of the large round bed. He lay in the centre, enmeshed in a black silk sheet, only the top of his head showing. She tiptoed over and saw that he was dead to the world.

'Mr Dexter,' she said firmly, 'it's time to wake up.'

There was no answer and she repeated the request. There was still no answer and she bent closer. What a perfect profile he had, and how incredibly thick his eyelashes were. It would serve him right if she pulled one sharply. He stirred and she drew back hastily. But it was only a movement in his sleep, and one bare, bronzed arm and shoulder came momentarily into view before disappearing again. Warmth suffused Robyn's face as she realised he was sleeping in the nude. She should have guessed it.

Retreating to the window, she drew another deep breath and pulled the curtains apart. Sunshine, bright as the Koh-i-noor diamond, flooded the bedroom.

'What the hell!' came a furious roar. 'Kim! Draw those damn curtains, will you?'

'It isn't Kim, Mr Dexter,' said Robyn, clear as a bell, and just as ringingly. 'It's Miss Barrett.'

The figure in the bed jack-knifed into a sitting position, and bleary eyes stared at her.

'What are you doing in my bedroom at this ungodly hour of the morning?' he demanded.

'Waking you up,' she said brightly. 'And it isn't an ungodly hour. It's half past seven.'

'Half past *what*? Have you gone out of your mind? Get out of here!'

'Only if you promise not to go to sleep again. We have a book to finish, Mr Dexter, and I like things done according to schedule. Everything planned, cut and dried.'

'You're mad,' he said in a flat voice. 'Quite mad. Are you sure you're Morton's secretary and not some escaped lunatic from a mental hospital?'

Robyn treated this remark with the disdain it merited. 'You gave Mr Phillips your word that you'd finish this book, Mr Dexter. Or is it true that when a *man* gives his word, he only means it at the time, and anyone who thinks otherwise is a fool?'

Bradley Dexter looked puzzled. 'I seem to have heard that comment somewhere before.'

'It's one of your own,' Robyn said, hiding a smile. 'I just changed the sex.'

He sighed heavily, and with a lean hand raked his shiny black hair back from his forehead. 'What point are you trying to make, Miss Barrett?'

'Merely that everything you despise about *my* sex, I despise in *yours*. If I weren't such a great admirer of your books, Mr Dexter, I wouldn't stay here a single moment.'

'I don't see that as a threat,' he retorted, and gave a prodigious yawn. 'For God's sake go back to bed, will you.'

'You have twenty minutes to get dressed and come down to breakfast,' she answered. 'We have half an hour to eat, and half an hour for you to look at your post before we start work at nine.'

'What time are we planning to stop?'

'At noon—which I believe is French custom. But we begin again at two-thirty and continue until six—with a short break for tea.'

'The only liquid I drink is coffee or alcohol.'

'If we maintain this schedule,' Robyn went on as if he had not spoken, 'we should be able to complete your book in four weeks instead of six, which will enable me to leave here that much earlier.'

His eyes widened disbelievingly. 'Are you telling me you prefer working in an office to living a life of luxury in a millionaire's villa?'

'Yes, I am. Particularly when I don't like the millionaire!'

'What a pity,' he said, and throwing aside the sheet, bounded out of bed, as naked as the day he was born.

Robyn was too flabbergasted to show any reaction whatever. She looked at him as if she had been turned into a pillar of salt, and indeed she felt exactly like Lot's wife, except for the fact that she was still in Gomorrah.

'My God, you're a cool customer!' Bradley Dexter drawled, misinterpreting her stony expression and stance for one of indifference. 'Doesn't *anything* take you by surprise?'

Turning her back on him, Robyn walked to the door. 'Not a man's body,' she lied. 'I've seen too many! I'll meet you at breakfast, Mr Dexter. *Dressed.*'

Outside in the corridor, she leaned against the wall, her limbs shaking too much for her to walk. Regardless of what it meant to Morton Publishing, it was impossible for her to remain at the villa. She hurried back to her room, intent on putting as much distance as possible between herself and Mr Dexter. She would book her return flight to London and then pack.

It was only as she reached for the telephone that the humour of the situation struck her. Recollecting the way she had marched into his bedroom, ruthlessly awakened him and then proceeded to lay down the law, she was in no way surprised by his reaction. To be honest, had she been in his position, she might well have done the same thing!

She giggled, then began to laugh, falling back upon the bed and pressing the sheet against her mouth in case anyone should hear her. If only Mr Dexter had guessed how near he had come to giving her heart failure! Indeed, it was a wonder she hadn't collapsed at his feet.

Remembering her consternation as he had stood in front of her, as perfect a male specimen as the magnificent Greek statues she had admired last year in Athens, she thanked her lucky star that her very consternation had been her salvation, for he had mistaken her silence for blaséness and not shock.

Smiling at the thought, she stood up and smoothed her dress, a crisp pink cotton that brought out the golden glints in her silvery hair. No, she would not return to London—yet. She had managed to get the whip hand over this dreadful man, and she intended to ride him hard.

At eight o'clock, she was having breakfast in the leaf-shaded patio at the far side of the house. Here lay the vegetable garden and fruit trees, warmed by the early morning sun whose slanting rays picked out the pale yellow of lemons, glinting like nuggets of gold amidst glossy green foliage, and warming the ripening peaches that nestled against the mellow stone wall.

Kim, in black trousers and short-sleeved white shirt, served her with fresh orange juice, hot croissants and home-made apricot jam, all washed down by fragrant French coffee, the like of which she had never tasted. But of Bradley Dexter there was no sign. At nine o'clock he had still not put in an appearance, and her belief that she had won this round began to fade. She should have known better than to think she could get her own way so easily. Not sure what to do next, she wandered along to the terrace. She could not bring herself to return to his bedroom, yet was more determined than ever not to go back to London, defeated.

'Miss Barrett?' Kim's voice made her swing round. 'Mr Dexter waiting in study for you. Please to go up.'

With fast beating heart Robyn did as she was told. Outside the door of the study she paused to compose herself, then with a fixed smile on her face, she went in.

Bradley Dexter sat in a black leather chair by the window, his feet stretched out on a matching stool. He wore tight-fitting cotton trousers and a silk Lacoste shirt, also in black. He was impeccably shaved, with his hair sleeked back, still wet from the shower. Only his eyes, red-rimmed and bleary, gave away the night before.

'You're late,' he said. 'Two minutes, to be precise.'

'I was expecting to see you at breakfast.'

'I'm still having mine.' He reached out to a side table and she saw that he was drinking a Bloody Mary.

'There's nothing like drink for ageing a man,' Robyn said promptly. 'It coarsens the skin and puts bags under the eyes. Yet men still think it adds to their masculinity.'

'Another little gem of yours?'

'No, Mr Dexter, of yours! Though you actually go on to say that the only alcohol a woman should consume is champagne.'

'You seem to have made quite a study of my books.'

'I have. I told you I——'

'Forget it,' he said hastily, and set his glass down on the table. 'Can you use that?' he asked, waving to the word processor.

'I'm afraid not,' she said. 'But I'm a fast typist, or I can take down your dictation in shorthand, which would be even quicker for you.'

'But you'd still have to transcribe it.'

'It's *your* time that's more valuable, Mr Dexter.'

Robyn went over to the desk and took out a shorthand pad and several pencils, glad she had had the foresight to come here last night to make sure she knew where everything was. Aware of him watching, she was hard put to it not to fumble, then determinedly thought herself back into the role she was playing—Miss Liberated Woman, 1990. Composedly she sat down and rested the pad on her knee.

'You know, Miss Barrett,' he said conversationally, 'you're too beautiful to be working as a secretary.'

'That's what all my employers say. But I happen to enjoy it.'

'I'm sure you could find other work that you'd enjoy even more.'

'You mean as a rich man's girl-friend? That isn't what *you* advocate, Mr Dexter. In every one of your books you say that the most important thing in life is to have work you enjoy doing, and that sex should be a pleasant pastime which should never take precedence.'

'That's true,' he said, after a moment's pause. 'But I've never met a woman who's agreed with me.'

'You have now.' She half lifted her pencil. 'I'm ready when you are.'

'But only for work,' he said slyly, and swung his feet to the ground.

The material stretched tightly across his thighs and though aware of it, Robyn made herself look at him with wide eyes.

'How predictable you are, Mr Dexter. You disappoint me. I thought you were different from other men.'

'I am different,' he smiled. 'I never have women secretaries.'

'I didn't realise it was because you were afraid.'

'Afraid of what?'

'That your lust would overcome your good sense.'

He burst out laughing. 'I don't think I'll have that fear with you, Miss Barrett. You're so damned matter-of-fact you'd turn off a ram in rut!'

Try as she would, Robyn could not keep a straight face, and her own laughter rang out.

'That's better,' said Bradley Dexter. 'I was beginning to think you had no sense of humour.'

'I have an excellent sense of humour,' Robyn said, reverting to her part again. 'It's important to cultivate one if you want to keep a man at arm's length. The male of the species doesn't like being laughed at.'

'Shall we start work?' her employer said, with a heavy sigh, and Robyn hid a smile and lowered her head to her notebook.

No matter how much she could fault Bradley Dexter's personal life-style, Robyn found it impossible to do other than admire the way he worked. She had met many authors during her two years with Morton Publishing, and knew that some liked to write in longhand, some created directly on to a typewriter, while others used dictaphones. But she had never met one who worked so fluently and concisely with a secretary. It was almost as if he were reading from an invisible page held up in front of him, so error-free was the fast flow of his dictation. Occasionally she wondered whether he had made notes beforehand, but when she stopped him at one point to query something, it set him off at a tangent and gave him an idea for an article, which he then dictated to her with the same fluency before returning, some three-quarters of an hour later, to his book.

At twelve o'clock, when she suggested they stop for a rest, he dismissed the idea, and continued with his dictation until two o'clock, when Kim wheeled in a trolley containing champagne in a silver ice-bucket, a mound of glittering caviar, surrounded by wedges of lemon, and a plate heaped high with hot buttered toast.

'I'm glad we're stopping for a little snack,' Robyn said coolly, vowing not to let him know how impressed she was.

'The sort of snack you have every day in London?' he enquired dryly.

'I could have if I wanted it,' she lied. 'But it would mean going out with older men. They're generally the only ones who can afford caviar.'

'Don't you know any successful *young* ones?'

'Not *that* successful.' She accepted a goblet of champagne and sipped it appreciatively. 'You're unique, Mr Dexter.'

'That's the first compliment you've paid me.'

'I've paid you at least a dozen,' she said. 'Each time I quote your books I'm complimenting you.'

'You have the ability to make a compliment sound like an insult!' He heaped a plate with caviar and passed it over to her. 'Since my looks and charm don't seem to be getting anywhere with you, perhaps the way to your heart is through your stomach!'

Robyn gave him a sweet smile. It was one that generally produced a glassy-eyed look in her male escorts, but Bradley Dexter was made of sterner stuff, and the only sign he gave was to move his eyes indolently over her face, as if he were making an inventory of each feature.

'I'm afraid you could never find your way to *my* heart, Mr Dexter,' she said. 'Though you have everything to recommend you to a woman—apart from being faithful and loyal to her, that is—which wouldn't bother me, of course, because I don't believe in that nonsense either—but unfortunately I don't get that special zing when I look at you.'

'Perhaps a little more champagne would help?'

'Do you like your women drunk and incapable, then?'

He plonked the champagne bottle hard into the ice, and returned to his chair. 'Shall we continue working?' he said.

Although still hungry, Robyn set her plate aside and picked up her pen.

She had no chance to put it down again until four-thirty, when the man in front of her rose, stretched his six-foot-three-inch frame, and announced that he had finished for the day.

'I suggest you get that typed back for me tonight,' he said, 'and I'll have a look at it in the morning. That means I won't start until about ten-thirty.'

'My working hours are nine till six,' Robyn informed him. 'I only work overtime if there's an emergency.'

'I thought there *was* an emergency over this book.'

'Mr Phillips expects it to be finished in six weeks, and at the pace I've allotted us, we should finish it in four.'

'At my pace we could do it in three; then you'd be shot of me, which would obviously make you happy.'

Robyn thought quickly. What a clever brute he was! But not quite clever enough.

'I'd be more than delighted to be shot of you, Mr Dexter,' she said primly. 'But I have prepared myself for four weeks in the sun, minimum, and I have no wish to cut it short. Besides, I enjoy caviar and champagne.'

For the second time that day he gave a roar of laughter. It was a warm, uninhibited sound, and she was hard put to it not to join in. But resolutely she didn't, and stared down at the floor until he was silent.

'I don't think you should work on until six today,' he said unexpectedly. 'You didn't have a proper break at lunchtime, so you might as well stop now and have a swim. You can spend tomorrow typing back what I've dictated, and I'll resume work the day after.'

The door closed behind him, and only then did Robyn slump back in her seat and drop her notebook to the floor.

CHAPTER THREE

THAT night Mrs Kim prepared a Vietnamese meal and Robyn enjoyed the pungent aroma of lemon grass, spices and chillis—though she was wary of this little red pepper, knowing from previous experience in a Thai restaurant that it could burn one's tongue like fire.

After dinner they sat on the little patio adjoining the kitchen, while Kim regaled her with stories of his life before he had been rescued from poverty by the man for whom he now worked. It seemed that Bradley Dexter had gone to a great deal of trouble and expense to get Kim and his wife out of the country, and though Kim saw it as a sign of the man's kindness, Robyn was not as certain. After all, in helping the Vietnamese couple, the author had also helped himself to the services of a loyal and hardworking pair who seemed willing to stay with him for the rest of their lives. True, he had offered to train Kim for any job he wanted, but this could have been an empty gesture—one which he knew Kim would not accept. Robyn wondered why she was so quick to dismiss Bradley Dexter's gesture of kindness, and decided that her antipathy for the man made it difficult for her to be unbiased. It was also far safer not to like him.

It was midnight before she returned to her room and, exhausted by her long day, fell fast asleep.

A delicious smell of coffee awakened her, and she lazily opened her eyes to see Mrs Kim setting a small silver tray and coffee pot on to a table beside the bed. Robyn's eyes went instantly to the clock and she gasped. It was after nine.

'Oh, lordy!' she cried. 'I forgot to set the alarm. Mr Dexter will wonder what's happened to me.'

'Mr Dexter no home.'

'You mean he's gone out already?'

'He no come back last night.'

'Oh.' Robyn had no need to ask why, and thought instantly of the redheaded nymphet with whom he had been cavorting in the pool on her first day here.

'Does Mr Dexter often stay out all night?' she asked casually.

'He stay out more since he meet Miss Forrester. She his girl four weeks now. Very pretty.'

Four weeks. Robyn was surprised such a girl could last this long with him and was curious to meet her face to face.

'Well, even though Mr Dexter's not home, it's no excuse for me to be idle,' she said aloud, and quickly poured herself a cup of coffee. 'I won't have breakfast on the patio, Mrs Kim. But if I can have some more coffee and fruit in the study . . .'

'Is no good eat and work at same time.'

With a smile, Robyn shook her head, and hurried into the bathroom.

It was noon, and she was busy transcribing at the electric typewriter, when footsteps above her told her that Bradley Dexter had returned. She tensed nervously, not putting it past him to wander downstairs in the nude to see what she was doing. If he did, she would definitely leave.

The door above her opened and bare brown feet descended into eye view. She glimpsed long muscular legs and her fingers tightened on the keys, only relaxing as a flash of white showed her short briefs covering narrow hips and flat stomach. Then he was sauntering across the room to her, torso bare, the thick tangle of hair on his chest curling in wet ringlets.

'Managing to get it all back?' he asked, nodding at her notebook and not bothering to say good morning.

'I never have trouble with my shorthand,' she replied,

then added for good measure, 'I hope you slept well, Mr Dexter?'

'When I did sleep,' he said, straightfaced, 'it was *very* well.'

To her horror, Robyn felt a blush steal over her face. There was nothing she could do to stop it and she knew that the man had seen it too, for he chuckled.

'Now why should a liberated lady be blushing? I thought you'd be unshockable.'

'I'm not blushing,' she denied, saying the first thing that came into her head. 'I changed colour because I was angry.' She saw from one raised eyebrow that he was waiting for her to explain, and wildly improvised, 'I don't like discovering that my hero has feet of clay, Mr Dexter, and that you're allowing a mere woman to come between you and your work.'

'I'm not,' he said, coming nearer to pick up some of the pages she had already typed. 'I told you I wasn't going to work until you'd typed all my shorthand back, which looks as if it will be tomorrow at the earliest.'

'Probably the day after,' she admitted. 'But surely you could be correcting the manuscript and making notes for the rest of it?'

'Are you presuming to tell me how I should write?'

The extreme gentleness of his voice warned her that she had trodden on dangerous ground, and knowing she was in the wrong, she gave him a winning smile.

'I'm sorry, Mr Dexter. You're right.' She turned back to the typewriter.

'Does that mean I have your permission to take the next two days off?' he enquired silkily.

'You're perfectly free to do as you like, so long as you don't——' Deliberately she stopped, dangling her sentence in mid-air like a worm in front of a fish.

'Provided I don't what?' he asked sharply, rising to the bait.

'Don't spend all your time with the same woman. That

would be going against one of your cardinal rules. "Play the field",' she quoted, ' "and never allow one female— no matter how enticing—to think she rules the roost". I expected to see you surrounded by little chicklets,' Robyn added for good measure.

'You're determined to make sure I practise what I preach, aren't you?' There was faint irascibility in his voice, but Robyn pretended not to notice it.

'Only because I can't bear the thought of you falling in love and being made to eat your own words.'

'There's no fear of that.' He moved to the spiral stair-case. 'The woman isn't born who can hold my interest on a permanent basis.'

'Does your present girl-friend know that?'

'All my girl-friends know it. They read my books as carefully as you do. Though unlike you, they all believe they can change my mind.'

'One of them might, if they catch you in a weak moment,' she warned. 'You said it yourself in——'

'My last book,' he finished for her.

She nodded. 'I've proof-read them all since I've been with Mr Phillips, and I know many paragraphs by heart.'

It was a good thing she had brought his last three books with her, Robyn thought, having decided it was politic to read them through carefully in case he referred to them. But never had she realised she might be using them as a rod to his back. Her lips quirked, and there was nothing she could do to prevent them curling into a smile. What fun she would have recounting some of these scenes to her friends!

'Are you laughing at me?' Bradley Dexter asked. 'I can assure you Holly doesn't have a snowflake's chance in hell of capturing me.'

'I'd believe it if she wasn't the only flower in the vase.'

'Then I'll pick another one for you,' he answered, and bounded up the stairs before she could think of a suitable reply.

Robyn did not see Bradley Dexter to speak to for the rest of the day. It was late in the afternoon before he left his room to take a swim in the pool, executing a perfect dive that left her gasping with envy as she watched him through the window in the study. He might burn the candle at both ends, she mused, seeing him plough cleanly through the water, length after length, but he had a long way to go before he reached the middle and finally burned himself out.

At seven she was in her room, resting and wondering whether to take herself out to dinner in Antibes that evening, when a high-pitched giggle floated up from the terrace below. Robyn ignored it, but when it came again, curiosity got the better of her and she peeped through the window. Drat it! She'd forgotten the terrace was covered in, and she could see nothing.

'Darling, you promised!' she heard a girl say, and though Bradley Dexter replied to it, his voice was too low to be audible to an eavesdropper.

Guiltily, Robyn backed away. What had happened to all her principles since coming here? What Mr Dexter did in his own time was his own affair. Staying cooped up in the villa like this was turning her into one of those females who lived vicariously through the lives of others. I'll take myself out for the evening, she decided, and reached for one of her new dresses, a crystal-pleated voile, high at the throat, but sleeveless, edged with blue satin a shade deeper than the dress itself. High-heeled blue suede shoes and bag completed her outfit, and on an impulse she unwound her hair from its loose coil on the nape of her neck and let it fall on either side of her face. Unconfined, it rippled to her shoulders like gilded satin, making her look, with her almond-shaped eyes and provocatively darkened lashes, like a sophisticated Botticelli angel—slimline version.

Smiling at the thought, she went downstairs. Only as she reached the hall did she realise she had no transport, and she went into the kitchen to ask Kim if there was a car available for her to use.

'Small Fiat in garage,' he replied, looking up from some silver he was polishing in the butler's pantry. 'I ask Mr Dexter, but I sure is okay.'

The Vietnamese disappeared, returning a few moments later to say his master wished to see her.

Schooling her expression to one of indifference, Robyn crossed the vast living room to the terrace. Soft lights turned it into a fairytale bower. Although the roof was covered, cool air wafted through the Moorish shaped archways, bringing with it the perfume of the sea that lay some two hundred feet below them, beyond the expanse of lawn that stretched away on the far side of the swimming pool. Not that she could see the pool from here. For that she would need to walk to the edge of the terrace, and right now she found she was trembling too much other than to stand still and look at the man who had summoned her.

He was as casually dressed as she had come to expect. His slacks were navy this time, worn with a dark red silk knit sweater that showed every muscle of his broad chest and shoulders. A red devil, she thought, and believed it to be confirmed when he gave her a mocking smile and reached out to clasp the scarlet-tipped hand of the lovely creature perched on the settee beside him.

'Holly, I'd like you to meet my new secretary, Miss Barrett.'

A beautiful, vacant face stared in Robyn's direction. Yes, it was the redhead, as she had suspected, and much younger than she had thought. Not more than eighteen, though there was very little dew left on her, if one could go by the pout of the mouth and the knowing look in the pale eyes.

'*Miss* Barrett?' she emphasised, and turned on the man next to her with a little shriek. 'You said it was a man!'

'I said my new secretary's name was Robyn,' he replied

in an amused tone. 'But don't let it worry you, angel, she thinks like a man. Don't you, Miss Barrett?'

'I try my best,' Robyn asserted. 'Did you wish to talk to me about the Fiat, Mr Dexter?'

'No. You can borrow it any time you like. I only wanted to know what your plans were for tonight. Morton called a short while ago and reminded me that I'm responsible for you while you're here.'

'Did he give you any message for me?' she asked, praying he had been careful not to give her away.

'All he did was warn me not to be taken in by your angelic appearance. Not that I would have been,' he added. 'You make yourself crystal clear.'

'Crystal clear about what?' Holly asked petulantly, wriggling herself closer to him, every delectable curve visible in a form-fitting silk jersey jump suit, underneath which she clearly wore nothing.

'That she's the male equivalent of myself,' Bradley Dexter replied.

'No one could be as cold-blooded as you, darling,' Holly giggled.

'Miss Dhimpoh to see you, sir,' Kim's voice intervened, and with a bound Bradley Dexter leapt from the settee to greet the slender, black-haired girl gliding towards them.

Singapore Airlines come to life, Robyn thought amusedly, and wondered if this man was a relation of Hugh Hefner, owner of *Playboy*, whose penchant for attracting some of the world's most beautiful women was well known.

'Mai! It's great to see you,' Bradley was now saying. 'How did you get here so quickly?'

'I took the first plane from Paris, as you instructed me,' she smiled, showing tiny white teeth, gleaming like little pearls, between a beautifully shaped mouth, painted fuller than it really was. She was olive-skinned, with slanting dark eyes, her exotic appearance enhanced by the high-necked, long-skirted tunic she wore. It covered every curve, yet disclosed them too, as she came nearer her host and put her two hands together in an attitude of prayer and lowered her head to them; a typical greeting of the Far East.

Bradley Dexter responded by drawing her into his arms as gently as if she were a lotus petal, and leading her to a two-seater love-seat, solicitously finding a stool for her feet—she barely reached his shoulder—then sitting himself beside her.

Well, well, Robyn thought. So our wolf can pretend to be a lamb when it suits him. It was an interesting discovery, for she would have thought Bradley Dexter too arrogant to pretend to be what he was not. Or perhaps he just put on an act until he'd got what he wanted? But from the way Miss Almond Eyes was looking at him, Robyn thought he had had it many times before. She wondered why he had sent to Paris for the girl, and was not left long in doubt, for as she murmured goodnight and went to the garage in search of the Fiat, she suddenly found him beside her.

'I hope you're pleased that I took your advice?' He stopped her with a detaining hand.

'My advice?'

'That there's safety in numbers.' His hand rose and touched her silky hair. 'With your colouring you'd be a much better foil for Mai than Holly.'

'But not as pliable,' Robyn retorted, and went towards the car.

Somehow the thought of Bradley Dexter with two lovely girls in tow spoiled what might otherwise have been a pleasant evening. She had never been to this part of the coast, and she spent an hour exploring the little town, with its delightful central square and broad main avenue leading down to a new esplanade, with towering apartment blocks—mark of the new developments springing up everywhere along this coastline. But she particularly liked the old part of the town, with its maze of ancient cobbled streets, narrow-windowed houses, shuttered to prying eyes, and the busy harbour, once a tiny port below the military barracks of Fort Carré, and now an expanding glittering marina, filled with opulent yachts.

She ate dinner in one of the restaurants overlooking the port. It was crowded with tourists and she felt rather alone. But the food was good and the half bottle of wine she consumed induced a feeling of lethargy and well-being.

Bowling up the drive to the villa, she heard the soft strains of music, and as she entered the house she knew from the sound of splashing and laughter that Bradley Dexter and his two lovely ladies were in the pool.

Trying to close her ears to their laughter, she went to bed, and was suddenly pleased that she had remembered to bring some ear-plugs with her. She put them in and immediately all sound ceased. But though she could blank out noise, she could not blank out the pictures flitting before her mind's eye, and she finally took out the plugs, switched on the light, and sat up to read.

Almost at once she heard voices along the corridor, and it required no imagination to guess where they were heading. The door to the lower wing opened and closed and Robyn found that her fingers were tightly clenched about the book she was holding. So he really did practise what he preached! She was consumed by a deep sense of disgust, the more strong because, for a short while today, she had entertained the belief that he might not have meant everything he had written.

Tossing her book aside, she went to sit by the window. The scent of night stock wafted up to her, as did the call of a lone cicada pleading for a mate. Pensively she wondered if she would ever find one of her own. Perhaps if she were plain-looking she might have attracted a different kind of man, but so far most of the ones she had met, though willing to marry her, did not possess the intensity and seriousness for which she was looking. She sighed gustily, and as the sound died away she heard footsteps running down the corridor and noisy sobs.

Quietly opening her door and, running out, Robyn saw Holly racing down the marble staircase. As the girl reached the bottom she looked up, expecting to see the man she had just left, but seeing Robyn instead, she gave an angry shriek.

'That swine!' she screeched. 'I don't play third wheel to anybody!'

She stormed out and Robyn sombrely returned to her room. Bradley Dexter was ... Words failed her, though they spun round chaotically in her brain, making sleep tedious to court.

The next morning she was not surprised to learn that Mai Dhimpoh was in residence, and for the next few days Bradley Dexter devoted himself exclusively to her. He acted like a child with a new toy; he was constantly beside the girl, swimming with her, dancing with her and at mealtimes happily letting her feed him from her plate.

Robyn tried to keep out of their way, but was drawn to watching them like a needle to a magnet. As one day led to another, and he still made no move to return to work, her anger mounted. Not that it wasn't wonderful to be staying here. It was almost like being sole guest in a five-star hotel. Until noon she had the swimming pool to herself, and could lie on one of the mattresses sunbathing without fear of being seen. For some reason she did not want to have Bradley Dexter's lascivious eyes upon her, or be forced into maintaining her pose with him; added to which she had taken a dislike to his new girl-friend since she had come into the kitchen and found her berating Mrs Kim for not serving them with lobster the night before. The voice, always dulcet when speaking to Bradley

Dexter, had been harsh, though it had given way to sweet sibilance as she had seen Robyn, and she had quickly walked out. Mrs Kim turned back to the table, where she was chopping mushrooms, but not before Robyn saw the telltale glitter of tears in her eyes.

'Don't let her upset you,' she had said impulsively, putting her slender arms around the woman's shoulders. Mrs Kim was no taller than Mai, and Robyn's five feet six inches without shoes towered over her. 'I'm sure Mr Dexter didn't mind not having lobster last night, and he'd be furious if he knew Miss Dimpoh had come in here giving you orders.'

'Please, you no tell him,' Mrs Kim said quickly. 'I no wish make trouble.'

'I know you don't,' Robyn assured her, but decided it was now time that she herself did.

Yet she was not quite sure exactly how to set about it, and two days passed, until here she was, floating on the cool water and staring up at the cloudless blue sky once again. Five days and not a stroke of work done. Was Mr Dexter always like this when he was with a new woman?

She swam to the side and clambered out, squeezed her hair as dry as she could and stretched out on a mattress, tilting the parasol above her so that her body was shaded from the sun. For a natural blonde she was extremely lucky to tan so easily, but she knew better than to try her luck too far, and was more than satisfied for her skin to be the colour of honey. It made her hair look more silver than gold, which in turn made her grey eyes look darker; shadowed pools that mirrored her growing anxiety at the thought of the small batch of manuscript that had been done since her arrival here.

She twisted over on to her stomach and unclasped the top of her bikini. Her breasts, rounded and full, flattened slightly as she lay on them and bared her back to the sun. A butterfly came to rest just within her vision, its wings wafting to and fro, giving her a tantalising glimpse of lilac and blue. Then it fluttered away, but the lilac colour returned in the form of the minuscule bikini that barely covered the Singapore girl's tiny figure.

Even eyeing her critically, one had to admit she was a beauty in miniature, but Robyn could not forget how hard the delicate face had become when focusing on Mrs Kim. She might be sweetness and light on the surface, but she was vinegar beneath. Just the sort of woman Bradley deserved—but not if it was going to prevent him finishing this book. But how could one get him to resume work?

The object of her thoughts padded out of the house, soft-footed as a panther and equally dark and sleek. His skin was like mahogany, and had a natural shine that needed no oil. He looked refreshed and at ease, as well he might, not having risen until a few minutes ago.

He sprawled down on a mattress and Kim immediately came into sight carrying the inevitable ice bucket of champagne. But this time it was accompanied by open-faced smoked salmon sandwiches and gulls' eggs.

'Would you like a glass of champagne, Miss Barrett?' Mai asked her prettily.

Robyn would have liked to refuse, but the thought of a drink was too tempting. Holding her bikini, she sat up, then turned her back on them both as she hooked the halter top into position.

'Shy?' Bradley Dexter asked behind her.

'Too sunburnt,' she replied, and swivelled round again to sit crosslegged on the mattress a few feet away from him.

Objectively he studied her, making no pretence of doing anything else. With an insouciance she did not feel, Robyn allowed him to do it, and at the same time watched him stare for stare. He was well worth looking at, but she made her expression bored as she turned her eyes away from him. He reached for the champagne bottle, the powerful biceps in his arms swelling as he did, then replenished Mai's glass and rose to do the same to her.

'You have an excellent figure, Miss Barrett,' he said conversationally, 'and a big bust for such a slender girl. Nice,' he added.

Silently she sipped her drink and he returned to his own mattress.

'It's *my* turn to be complimented,' said Mai with a little girl pout.

'I do that with action, not words,' he replied, and pulled her towards him.

'Mind the champagne!' she warned with a tinkling laugh as the bubbling liquid spilled across her golden-skinned stomach.

'Makes you all the tastier,' he murmured, and bent his head to lick her.

Without knowing why, Robyn was convinced he was doing it deliberately to irritate her. It was a good sign and showed he was not as immune to her opinions as he pretended. If she could only make him feel guilty at his idleness, she might even be able to persuade him to start work again.

'What about doing a couple of hours' dictation, Mr Dexter?' she suggested.

'Ask the boss.' He slanted an eye in Mai's direction.

Graceful the girl leaned towards him, the points of her breasts pressing against his chest.

'Do whatever makes you happy, Brad.'

'You mean you won't mind if I disappear for the rest of the day?'

'Not if it's what you wish.'

'It will mean cancelling our flight to Corsica.'

'You're the one in command,' Mai replied, her doe eyes looking at him with adoration.

'I wouldn't dream of disappointing you,' he said swiftly,

and stood up. 'I'm afraid it's no go, Miss Barrett. If Mai
had put up a fight you might have won, but as it is . . .'
He leaned down and planted a kiss on the other girl's
dark head. 'Be ready to leave in an hour, sweetheart. I'm
just going to telephone Martin and see how he's making
out.'

He strode away, leaving Robyn and Mai alone.

'Giving in to Brad is the best way of getting what you
want,' Mai said in her tinkling voice. 'But none of the
other girls in his life have ever realised it. He's like a
child. If you resist him he becomes more obstinate. But if
he believes he's in charge, he's malleable as butter.'

'What would you have done if he'd taken you at your
word and decided to do some work?' Robyn asked curiously.

'Nothing. I'm not yet in a position with him to do anything.'

'I take it you're hoping?'

'With Brad one can only hope.' She held out her hand,
and Robyn saw that her wrist was encircled by a narrow,
diamond-studded band. It was a delicate trifle, the more
expensive because of it, and Robyn knew instantly who
had bought it. 'Each day he gives me something different,'
Mai smiled. 'So it's worth giving in to him, don't you
think—even if one knows it can never lead to anything
permanent.'

Robyn admired the girl for her honesty, though not for
her greed.

'Mr Dexter has to finish a book,' she said abruptly. 'It's
very important for the publishers I work for. That's why
my boss sent me here.'

'I know. Bradley told me.'

'If you could encourage him to work for part of each
day, I'm sure we'd be able to get it done in time.'

'Brad can't do things by halves,' said Mai. 'He might
say he'd only work for half of each day, but once he started

there'd be no stopping him, and the next thing would happen is that he'd send me away. He hates distractions when he's working.'

'Even if he asked you to go, it would only be for four weeks—maybe less if I worked overtime. Then you could come back again.'

Mai shook her head. 'That isn't Brad's style. Once he stops seeing you, he's more likely to become interested in a new face, not renewing acquaintance with an old one.'

And a new body, Robyn thought glumly, though aloud she said: 'When you first came here I had the impression you'd known Mr Dexter before.'

'Not in the sense *you* mean. I was a close friend of Prince Bunthar, who was a great friend of Brad's.'

'Wasn't he killed at Le Mans last year?' Robyn asked, vaguely recollecting having read of the Burmese prince's fabulous wealth and lifestyle.

'Yes, and Brad was a great comfort to me. Then he went off to the States and I never heard from him. I was quite surprised when he called me in Paris and invited me to come down here.' The girl nestled back among the pillows. 'I hope you see why I can't do as you ask, Miss Barrett? If I did, and he sent me away, I'd be jeopardising my chances.' Mai fingered the circlet of diamonds around her wrist in a way that gave point to her answer. 'It would please me very much if you didn't keep asking Brad to start work. He'll finish the book when he's ready—and that won't be until I've left here; which may be quite a while.' The girl half smiled. 'You know, it might be better for everyone if *you* went away. You could always come back again when you're needed.'

Robyn controlled her anger. 'I've no intention of leaving without the book.'

'Then you might have a long wait.' Mai rose. 'I'll see you when we get back from Corsica.'

She undulated away and, feeling thoroughly fed up,

Robyn plunged into the pool. She had no idea how long Bradley Dexter would be away, but knew it was unwise to ask him. If he only planned to stay in Corsica a day, devilment might make him extend it. Idly she wondered if she had been overplaying her hand with him. Maybe her assertiveness was making him more obstinate. Perhaps it was a case of 'Softly, softly catchee monkey'. After all, being Miss Sweetness and Light was paying off for Mai, so why not for herself too?

All at once Robyn felt better. When Bradley Dexter returned from Corsica he would find a changed secretary waiting for him.

CHAPTER FOUR

IT was three long, sun-filled, yet tedious days before Bradley and Mai returned to the villa. Robyn had had time to formulate her plan, and knew she had to be subtle about it. She was too tall to be able to copy Mai's physical mannerisms, but there was no reason why she shouldn't mimic her docile attitude and deference. With two adoring females flapping around him, she was banking on Bradley Dexter's intelligence to guess the point she was trying to bring home to him.

'I hope you didn't find it too boring being on your own?' he asked, coming down to the pool to find her.

He looked, if anything, browner than when he had gone away, and disgustingly healthy. Passion-filled nights obviously agreed with him, she thought waspishly, and bit back a sharp answer.

'It's been wonderfully peaceful here,' she replied. 'I feel as if I'm on holiday.'

'Has Morton phoned for me?'

'He rang *me* to find out how things were going.'

'I'm sure you told him!'

'I said you were busy entertaining a foreign visitor, but that you'd make up the lost time as soon as you could.'

Hazel eyes glinted at her. 'Are you being serious?'

'I don't joke about business.' Robyn looked at him with pretended earnestness. 'I owe you an apology, Mr Dexter. While you were away, I've been re-reading your books and——'

'Not that again!'

'Please hear me out,' she begged. 'I should have realised from the start that you don't like being ordered around any more than I do. And of course, you've *more* right to be your own master. You've made a brilliant success of your life, and if you don't want to write any more, it's no one's concern except your own. It was my loyalty to Mr Phillips that prevented me from realising it.'

'I'm not without loyalty myself, Miss Barrett,' he answered sharply. 'Morton's a good friend of mine and I don't want to let him down.'

'One's first loyalty is to oneself,' Robyn stated.

'Dammit, you're quoting me again!'

'Am I?' she asked with lying innocence. 'I hadn't realised.'

'We'll continue with the book tomorrow,' he promised suddenly. 'I'll have a word with Mai.'

Knowing that if he did, he definitely wouldn't work, Robyn nodded and watched him stride away. Well, she'd made herself into a doormat and all he'd done was tread on her. Still, she wasn't going to abandon the act yet. There were a few more cards left to play.

At the terrace, he turned and called out to her.

'We'll be in for dinner tonight, Miss Barrett. I'd like you to join us.'

'Thank you, Mr Dexter, I'd be delighted.'

That night Robyn dressed with care. Her outfit was as near to one of Mai's high-necked traditional dresses as she could find, and it had required assiduous searching for in the Nice boutiques. It was the same silver-grey as her eyes, with delicate pink roses embroidered across the bodice, and down the long slit in the straight skirt.

She drew her hair back from her face and combed it into a high roll, keeping it in place with little jewelled combs. Her make-up was minimal, except for her eyes, which she darkened and elongated. High-heeled sandals and a liberal spray of perfume completed the picture. All she needed to do now was to walk as if she were gliding, and to practise a decorous pose.

Bradley Dexter and Mai were already in the living

room when she entered, and Robyn was taken aback to see the girl's outfit was almost a mirror image of her own. But in pink with grey flowers instead of the other way around.

The man was quick to notice it too, and he grinned at them both.

'You girls aren't ganging up on me, are you?'

Mai looked puzzled, and since humour did not seem to be a forte of any of his girl-friends, Robyn answered the question.

'If you'd prefer me to change into something else, Mr Dexter, it won't take me a moment.'

'Not at all, you look charming—both of you!' He reached for a cheroot and Robyn hurriedly picked up a lighter and flicked it on for him.

Surprised, he lit up, then blew a cloud of smoke. As it came her way she did not flinch, but stood impassively, head slightly bent as if in obeisance.

'Sorry about that,' he said, waving the smoke away from her.

She nodded gently and sat down, back erect, legs decorously crossed, the way she'd seen Mai sit.

At dinner Robyn emulated the girl too, taking small portions of food and still managing to leave half of it, as if she were too fragile to be anything as mundane as hungry; making little protesting sounds when Kim replenished her wine glass and giving a girlish laugh when champagne was served with the iced apricot soufflé.

'You're the most lavish host in the world,' she breathed, and glanced at Mai. 'Don't you agree with me?'

'Of course,' Mai said shortly.

Bradley Dexter looked amused as his eyes met Robyn's. 'How come you're so lavish with your compliments tonight? Had a change of heart towards me, Miss Barrett?'

'I've realised that opinions formed on a prejudice are

unworthy ones,' she murmured, and saw a puzzled expression flit across his face; as if he knew something was going on, but was not quite sure what.

Mai, however, was in no doubt. She had known it from the moment Robyn had entered the room.

'I'm surprised your employer allowed you to come and work here,' she said now. 'Wasn't he worried in case you preferred to stay in France and not go back to London?'

'It isn't a question of what *I* prefer,' Robyn said sweetly. 'We both know Mr Dexter will never employ a woman secretary on a permanent basis.'

'I might be encouraged to change my mind,' he said, and reached for a cigar. 'Any objections if I smoke at the table?'

'I love the smell of cigars,' said Mai, breathing in deeply.

'This is your house,' Robyn added. 'And you're the master in it.'

Once again he looked puzzled, and she warned herself not to overplay her hand.

'If you'll both excuse me,' she said, pushing back her chair, 'I have a slight headache and I think I'll take a stroll in the garden.'

Gracefully she moved away, taking small steps and hearing her silk skirt rustle.

'Tomorrow at nine?' Bradley Dexter called after her. 'But I'll only work till noon.'

'That's very nice of you, Mr Dexter. I appreciate it.'

Hiding her triumph, Robyn went on to the terrace and, once out of sight, walked in her normal, easy way down to the next level. She loved the pool at night. The blue and green mosaic tiles made the water scintillate like a peacock's tail, iridescent in the floodlights that bathed the whole area.

A faint breeze had sprung up and it ruffled the silver tendrils of hair that had escaped the confining coil on the nape of her neck. She tugged at the high collar of her dress and wished she were wearing something low-cut and looser, but knew that tomorrow she would be wearing yet another Oriental type outfit. She half smiled. It was less amusing to play the part of a yes-woman than the other role she had assigned herself, but both parts were for the same reason: to bring about the downfall of the most supercilious, conceited man she had ever encountered.

A rustle behind her made her turn, and she saw Mai coming towards her. With no man to watch, the girl's expression was less than its usual serene one. In fact it was a downright militant one, and there was a hard, singularly unattractive gleam in the normally doe-like eyes. Robyn braced herself for the anger she knew was to come.

'You think you're very clever, don't you?' Mai hissed. 'Well, I won't let you get away with it!'

'With what?' Robyn asked guilelessly.

'With trying to fool Brad that you're the docile little secretary here to do his bidding.'

'That's exactly why I'm here,' Robyn answered. 'And may I remind you that Mr Dexter himself was the one who suggested we start work again?'

'Only because of the way you sucked up to him— laughing at all his jokes and deferring to everything he said, as if he were your lord and master!'

'We'll only be working in the morning,' Robyn placated. 'You can have him all to yourself in the afternoons—and the nights too,' she added.

Mai's face was tight with fury. 'Unfortunately it won't turn out that way. Once Brad starts writing he won't have time for anyone else. I told you what he was like before I went to Corsica with him—and I warned you not to try to come between us.'

'That the last thing I want to do,' Robyn assured her. 'But Mr Dexter does have a manuscript to finish, and it's my job to see he does so. I'm sorry you're upset about it, but there's nothing I can do.'

'There's something *I* can do,' Mai responded quietly, and hit Robyn sharply in the pit of her stomach, sending her toppling into the water.

With a startled cry Robyn put out her hands to save herself. But encumbered by high heels and a tight-fitting dress, she had no way of retaining her balance, nor of preventing her head from hitting the protruding edge of the swimming pool.

She felt herself going down, down into the blue-green depths, then rising again several yards away from the edge. Dazed by the blow, she was disorientated and started swimming in the wrong direction. Her dress weighed her down like a lead sack, wrapping itself around her legs and making it impossible for her to move them. She sank again, choking and swallowing water, then rose gasping for air.

She thought she heard someone shout her name and turned in the direction it came from. Mascara was burning her eyes and they were streaming with chlorinated water, which made it difficult to see through them. Valiantly she tried to swim towards the sound. There was a splash, and she saw a dark figure cleaving its way towards her, then strong arms were holding her and Bradley Dexter's voice was telling her to relax and that she was safe.

Strangely enough, she knew she was, and with a sigh she closed her eyes and let his hands support her head above the water as he drew her to the side of the pool. Only then did she try to lever herself out, but before she could manage it he swung her up into his arms and carried her with him.

He set her on her feet, but as she tried to stand, her legs gave way, and she would have crumpled to the ground had he not reached out and caught her again.

'I'm sorry,' she gasped. 'How silly of me! But I feel quite faint.'

'Your cheek's grazed,' he said in an angry voice. 'You've hurt your face.'

'I slipped,' she whispered, grateful for the feel of his arms about her. 'If you could put me in a chair, I'll soon get my breath back.'

'You'll soon get a chill too, if you don't get into some dry clothes.'

'I'll call Kim to take Miss Barrett to her room,' said Mai, bending forward sympathetically. 'Poor girl! It was foolish of her to wear such high heels. She must have tripped on one of the flagstones.'

Not bothering to reply, Bradley Dexter lifted Robyn into his arms again, as effortlessly as if she were a doll, and strode up the stone steps towards the house. Robyn rested against him, her wet head upon his sopping shirt. His feet squelched on the marble stairs, and she had a sudden picture in her mind of how ludicrous they must look, both dressed to the nines and dripping water.

'You'd better change too,' she ordered faintly.

'Even half drowned, you're still bossy!' he muttered, and kicking open her bedroom door, carried her straight into the bathroom and sat her on a towel-covered chaise-longue beside the bath. 'Stay where you are and don't move. I'll send Mrs Kim up to undress you and get you into bed.'

Robyn couldn't have moved if she had wanted, and she lay back in the chair, her head throbbing.

It was a relief to put herself in Mrs Kim's gentle, competent hands, though it was more than an hour later, after a warm bath and coffee laced with brandy, before she felt human again. Not that she had any intention of getting up, but she wanted to go over to the dressing table to look at the swelling she could feel on her face. She would probably have a nasty bruise there in the morning. She touched it gingerly, wincing as she did.

There was a knock at the door, but before she could say come in, Bradley Dexter stood there, with another older man in a brown linen suit, carrying a small attaché case.

'I called Dr Mercier,' he said abruptly, introducing the stranger. 'I want him to check you out.'

'There's nothing wrong with me,' Robyn protested. 'I'll be fine in the morning.'

'You may have slight concussion,' Dr Mercier interjected. 'And I'd like to look at that cut on your cheek.' He glanced at the frowning, dark-haired man beside him, who took the hint and went out. 'It's not pleasant to fall into a pool,' the doctor went on kindly. 'It's a shock to the system, *n'est-ce pas*?'

Robyn saw no reason to tell him she had been pushed, and merely nodded as he started to examine her. He paid particular attention to her vision, warning her she must let him know if she started feeling any head pains or nausea.

Promising she would, Robyn swallowed the two pills he gave her, and then lay back on the pillow.

She woke up once, somewhere near dawn, and heard a chair creak. Turning her head nervously, she was just able to make out the figure of a man sitting by the window. The silver-grey sky illuminated the jet black hair, and she half smiled.

'You shouldn't have sat up with me, Kim,' she murmured sleepily, and turned over on her side, somehow feeling pleased she was not alone.

The next time she awoke it was broad daylight and she felt almost her old self again, though she was careful to get out of bed slowly, before padding into the bathroom.

What a sight she looked! The top half of her cheek was a pretty shade of purple, though her eyes itself was unmarked. She had been lucky to have got off so lightly.

As she remembered Mai's hands thrusting at her, her feeling of relief ebbed, and more soberly she made herself tidy and returned to bed. She knew without being told that there would be no work for herself and Bradley Dexter this morning, which made Mai the winner of this particular round. The girl was going to be a bad enemy, and she must watch her step if she didn't want something more serious to happen to herself. It's like an Agatha Christie murder, Robyn thought, and the humour of the situation made her laugh out loud.

'I'm glad you've found something to amuse you!' Bradley Dexter said from the doorway, and she turned her head sharply as he came over to the bed. 'May I share the joke?'

'It wasn't a joke,' she said awkwardly, and went on looking at him.

He had not shaved, and stubble darkened the firm line of his jaw. Somehow it lessened the severity of it, giving him a dishevelled air that put her in mind of a castaway on an island. He was certainly dressed for the part, in fashionable frayed-edged shorts and a white singlet, through which the black hairs on his chest could clearly be seen.

'I slept very well,' she said quietly, before he had time to ask her. 'And I feel practically back to normal.'

'You've still got to stay in bed today,' he said abruptly. 'Doctor's orders, not mine. Mrs Kim will be bringing you breakfast in a moment, and if there's anything else you want, ring the bell.'

'Yes, sir,' Robyn smiled. 'And may I thank you for rescuing me last night?'

His shoulders lifted. 'I'd have done the same for anyone.'

It was a truthful answer, but not a particularly polite one, and she was glad when, without another word, he left the room.

Hardly had the door closed behind him when it opened again and Mrs Kim came in with her breakfast.

'You much better?' she asked, placing the tray across Robyn's lap.

'So much that I feel a fraud staying in bed. But Mr Dexter insists on it.'

'He clever man. You listen him.'

Robyn spooned a liberal portion of apricot jam on her croissant and bit into it. 'Please thank your husband for me,' she said. 'It was very kind of him to sit up with me during the night.'

Busily dusting the dressing table, Mrs Kim turned round in surprise. 'Is not my husband stay, Miss Barrett, is Mr Dexter. He very concerned in case you have concussion. I offer stay, but he no let me.'

Robyn's cheeks flamed. Although she had expected Bradley Dexter to be concerned—as her temporary employer he was responsible for any accident she might have on his premises—she had not anticipated him sitting with her himself, and she found his solicitude surprising. Yet it shouldn't be, for he had shown gentleness and understanding when he had carried her from the pool to her room. Because it was not a thought she wished to ponder on, she pushed it away and poured herself some coffee. Well, at least Mai would be pleased with herself today, for now she would have her boy-friend to herself. This thought was considerably less enjoyable than the previous one, and she pushed it away too.

'I think I'll sit by the window after I've had breakfast,' she said aloud.

'You stay in bed,' Mrs Kim replied firmly, 'or I tell Mr Dexter.'

Robyn grinned. 'Let him enjoy his day of freedom, Mrs Kim. Concussion or not, he'll be working with me tomorrow!'

'He working now. He by pool reading manuscript.'

Robyn's smile widened. 'Miss Dhimpoh won't like that.'

'She no here.' Mrs Kim was again industriously tidying the room. 'Mr Dexter send her packing.'

'Packing?' Robyn echoed. 'You mean he sent her away?'

Mrs Kim nodded. 'Last night, after doctor go, they

have big row. He say she push you in pool—he saw from window. Miss Dhimpoh cry no, but he shout yes. He very angry.'

Robyn heard this out in silence. She was delighted that Bradley Dexter had seen Mai's mean-spirited act, but astonished that he had sent the girl away. It was quite out of character with what he wrote. Having two women quarrelling over a man was excellent for the male ego, he had written. But perhaps the fact that her own desire to have him was not a personal one had affected his reaction. Yes, that was it. Still, it had been drastic of him to send his girl-friend packing.

Robyn kept returning to the thought for the rest of the day; and what a long, tedious one it was, broken only by Mrs Kim's entry with lunch, and tea.

At supper time Robyn resolutely refused to remain in her room any longer. But though determined to dress and go downstairs, she felt decidedly shaky by the time she reached the hall, and she perched on the last step to recover.

'Don't you *ever* do anything you're told?' a furious voice demanded behind her.

'Yes, Mr Dexter,' she replied, not looking round. 'But I don't like being cosseted unnecessarily. I'm perfectly well.'

'Oh, sure,' he snapped, still furious, and heaving her to her feet, frogmarched her into the living room, where he immediately let her go.

Luckily he had deposited her beside an armchair and she collapsed into it ignominiously. He stood watching her and, seeing the sudden smile twitching his mouth, it was impossible for her not to smile back.

'You're right,' she confessed. 'I suppose I should have listened to you. But I got fed up being alone in my room.'

'I assumed you'd be too self-sufficient to be bored with your own company,' he replied, sauntering over to the drinks trolley, and deftly uncorking a bottle of champagne. He poured out two glasses, came back to hand her one, and then sprawled on a settee facing her.

As usual he was casually dressed: all in blue tonight. It made his skin look even darker and his hair blue-black. He was far too good-looking to spend the rest of his life single and unattached. He should have someone to care for, who would also care for him.

What's the matter with me? Robyn wondered crossly. Just because he sat up with me last night, there's no reason to invest him with needs he doesn't have. Unexpectedly she found herself curious to find out whether he had always been so wary of women. Surely he had a mother somewhere whom she loved? And what about brothers and sisters? And his father? Unwilling to give free rein to her thoughts, she brought them firmly back to the present.

'I'd better go and tell Mrs Kim I've come down for dinner. If I——'

'She and Kim are out. They didn't want to go, but I insisted. There's a Vietnamese dance troupe playing in Nice, and they had tickets for it.'

'You mean we're alone?' The thought was unexpectedly alarming.

'Scared?' he mocked.

'No, Mr Dexter. Hungry. For food,' she added, seeing the gleam in his eye.

'That's what I figured.' Lithely he rose. 'Mrs Kim put your supper ready on a tray, so I can either bring it to you here or you can join me in the kitchen.'

'I'll join you,' she said, and stood up carefully.

He did not offer to help her, for which she was glad, and walked ahead of her to the kitchen, leaving her to follow him more slowly.

When she entered it, he had already wheeled a laden trolley on to the little patio and was setting the table. There was iced consommé, cold lobster salad and a bowl of fresh raspberries and cream. A tall bottle of hock, chilled so that a bloom lay upon it, stood next to two delicately fluted glasses.

'Not bad for the cook's night out,' Robyn quipped, sitting down.

'Do you object to luxury?' he questioned.

'Not if it's earned. And you've earned yours, Mr Dexter.'

'I'm glad you think so.' He began to eat. 'You rather gave me the impression that you thought my success came too early.'

'I think your books came too easily to you,' she said carefully, picking up her spoon. 'I mean I think you could write something far more difficult—but equally interesting—if you set your mind to it.'

'The definitive novel?'

'Why not? Haven't you wanted to?'

'Not yet. Perhaps one day I will.' His teeth gleamed as he smiled. 'When I'm old and grey I'll change my tune, but for the moment I enjoy dancing to it.'

'Are you never bored by its repetitiveness?'

'Are you?' he countered. 'You're how old, Miss Barrett? Twenty-two, twenty-three?—and if you're as great a disciple of my books as you say, you must have known many men. Are you telling me *you're* bored with them?'

Robyn swallowed a portion of the delicious jellied consommé which gave her a little more time to decide what to answer.

'Yes,' she said finally. 'That's why I've given myself another five years before I settle down and have a family.'

'I knew there was a nesting instinct deep down inside you!'

'I didn't say I was going to get married,' she retorted. 'Merely that I want to have children.'

He digested this remark with the rest of his soup, and

she was delighted to see she had flummoxed him. He was so convinced he knew everything there was to know about women that he found it difficult to believe that one of them could ever say something to surprise him. But she had a few more surprises in store, she thought mischievously, and was amazed how easy she was finding it to play this part. The world's lost a great actress in me, she decided, and said aloud:

'I could never imagine myself being content with one man. I need at least two.'

'Is that so?' he enquired. 'And may I ask who the present two are?'

Wildly she sought for an answer, but none came to mind. All she could think of was her current boy-friend, David, a pleasant, uninspiring young accountant her parents hoped she would marry.

'Of course not,' she answered, still desperately thinking. In the distance a car revved, and somewhere a dog barked, and went on barking—a high-pitched sound, like her mother's Scotties. Of course. The Scotties!

'At the moment I'm with Hamish and Alex,' she said.

'Scotsmen?'

'Without a doubt. Strong, short-tempered, but very lovable.'

'Handsome too, I suppose?'

'Would *you* waste time with an ugly girl?' Robyn did not wait for an answer. 'Hamish is very handsome. He has black curly hair and dark eyes. He loves going for long walks.'

'And Alex?'

'Older and not quite so energetic.'

'How much older?'

She multiplied each of Alex's years by seven, which was the popular way of humanising a dog. 'He's forty-nine,' she said casually.

'You're mad! That's far too old for you.'

'I don't see why you say that. You're thirty-four and Holly couldn't have been more than eighteen.'

Bradley Dexter's mouth half-opened and then clamped shut.

'What do they do?' he asked finally.

'Nothing.' Robyn was momentarily at a loss, then quickly recovered herself. 'Well—without boasting—they both come from a wonderful line. Highly pedigreed, you might say.'

'My God, you make them sound like a pair of dogs!'

'I don't call your girl-friends bitches!' she said indignantly. 'So there's no need for you to be insulting.'

'Sorry,' he replied, not bothering to look it. 'Does this Hamish, or whatever his name is, feature as a father for your children?'

'It's too early for me to say. Ask me that question in a few years' time.' She leaned forward and looked at him with great candour. 'Don't *you* want any children, Mr Dexter?'

'I don't have sufficient conceit to wish to perpetuate myself.'

'But children can be such fun.'

'Fun!' he said harshly. 'You don't have children for fun. They need to be cared for, worried over, listened to, loved. At every stage of their development they require your time and interest. If you aren't prepared to give them that—don't ever have any!'

It required no intelligence for Robyn to guess that his own childhood had been an unhappy, unloved one.

'Yes,' he said, abruptly, reading her expression, 'you're quite right. My arrival on this planet was an unwelcome accident which my mother did her best to forget.'

'And your father?'

'He loved her so much he was willing to do anything to keep her. Even to the point of abandoning me.'

'Oh no!' Robyn was aghast.

'Well, not in the accepted sense,' he admitted, helping himself to a large portion of lobster and motioning her to do the same. 'I was brought up by a nurse, sent off to boarding school when I was six, and remained there—even during the holidays—until I walked out at sixteen. The rest of my life I'm sure you know.'

She nodded. Dishwasher in a restaurant, merchant seaman for three years, and a whole host of other jobs until, at twenty-four, he had produced his first book, and been a success and a celebrity ever since.

'Where are your parents now?' she asked tentatively.

'Dead. They died as they lived, Miss Barrett, together and enjoying themselves. Sailing between the Bahamas and Barbados they were caught in a freak storm.'

There were many things Robyn wanted to say, but she knew better than to utter any of them. It was clear now why this man disliked women, blaming them all because of the behaviour of one. She understood, too, why he refused to succumb to love, and why he saw it as a terrible weakness—for love had made his own father weak. Yet there were many children who had been brought up without affection, yet had managed to lead normal lives and commit themselves to a relationship. Perhaps this man might have done the same had he not achieved such success with his first book. But advocating polygamy and becoming its chief spokesman, he had found no reason to disavow it; indeed, his continuing success had only made him more deeply entrenched in his opinions.

Never would he admit he was wrong; nor would he concede that he was psychologically damaged. To do that, he needed far greater self-awareness in order to recognise that he was capable of being much more than he was. But then why should he change? Handsome and rich enough to buy what he wanted, he had no reason to work at a relationship. In fact the word 'relationship' was one from which he shied away.

Surreptitiously Robyn regarded him. He was eating with blithe unconcern, as though he did not care that he had given himself away. Such an attitude could only come from supreme self-assurance, and it suddenly struck her that though he had been a hurt child and adolescent, he was in no way a hurt man. The shell he had built around himself had become a second skin— hard as titanium—and would remain with him for the rest of his life.

'What made you the way *you* are?' he asked unexpectedly, and she was so surprised by the question that she was not sure what he meant. 'It couldn't only be reading my books that made you see the light,' he went on. 'Did you have absent parents too?'

'On the contrary, they were genuinely doting. They still are. They've lavished everything on me, and I grew up with supreme self-confidence.'

'Knowing you were intelligent and exceptionally beautiful,' he stated, eyeing her with the candour of a diligent housewife inspecting a joint of meat at the butcher's. 'The only thing that spoils you, Miss Barrett, is your practical streak.'

'Aren't you practical?' she asked indignantly.

'Not when I'm laying siege to a woman.' Deftly he removed the plates and placed the bowl of raspberries between them. 'Then I can be as romantic as a lovesick swain—flowers, presents, the lot.'

'Until the citadel is conquered and you ride away in search of another one!'

'I leave no bleeding hearts behind me,' he mocked. 'The citadels I conquer are all there for the taking, and I make no promises I've no intention of keeping.'

'Where's Mai?' Robyn asked abruptly, disliking to hear him talk this way.

'She had to return to Paris. Urgent business.'

'You're lying,' Robyn stated. 'Mrs Kim told me you sent her away.'

'Only because her act was becoming a bore.' Hazel eyes suddenly lightened with humour. 'That was your doing, of course, Miss Barrett. Damn! I really can't keep calling you that.'

'I wondered if you'd noticed my behaviour,' she said demurely, placing the tips of her fingers together and lowering her head towards them in an obeisant attitude.

His chuckle was sufficient answer, and he made no other as he stacked the dishes on the trolley and wheeled it deftly into the kitchen.

'Coffee here or in the living room?' he called.

'I'll make it,' she said.

'No.' His voice was terse. 'I don't want you waiting on me.'

'You say that women should.'

'I say that girl-friends should,' he corrected. 'That doesn't apply to secretaries.'

Robyn should have been delighted at this, since it showed he no longer regarded her as a citadel to be conquered. But she was not pleased, and she was alarmed to realise it, admitting with her usual candour that this past hour in Bradley Dexter's company had made her see him with kinder eyes.

Too kind, in fact, because she saw the danger inherent in liking this man; knowing how quickly it could turn into something deeper. Hadn't Morton Phillips warned her about the warm Mediterranean nights?

'I don't think I'll have coffee after all,' she said hurriedly. 'I'm feeling tired and I'll go to bed.'

'No headache or dizziness?' he asked sharply.

'No, Mr Dexter. I assure you I don't have concussion.'

He relaxed and turned back to the percolator. 'Call me Brad,' he ordered over his shoulder. 'Each time you say

Mr Dexter it reminds me I have work to do.'

   'Then maybe I'd better go on doing it. If——'

   'Goodnight, Robyn,' he interrupted. 'Sleep well.'

   'Thank you. Goodnight—Brad.'

CHAPTER FIVE

ROBYN was down for breakfast before eight the next morning, but early though she was, she was too late to catch Bradley Dexter, who had left the villa a half hour before to fly to Rome.

'He leave message for you,' said Kim, handing her an envelope.

Convinced she had been left to kick her heels while Bradley enjoyed the *dolce vita*, Robyn tore open the envelope furiously, her anger abating as she read the firm, bold writing.

'I had a call last night from my aunt. She's in Rome for two days en route to San Francisco and this is my only chance of seeing her till the autumn. I expect to be back late tomorrow.' Beneath the sprawling signature was a P.S. 'She really is my aunt! A sprightly seventy-four-year-old who's the one and only female I give a damn about!'

Robyn put the letter into the pocket of her dress and wondered how to occupy herself for the next two days. Living the life of a lotus-eater was definitely not her scene, and she debated whether to go to Antibes and look around the shops or drive farther afield to Nice or Monte Carlo. It was only as the words Monte Carlo came into her mind that she remembered her friend Anna, with whom she had been at school, and had not seen since she had married a dishy-looking Frenchman three years ago, and left England.

She hurried to the phone book. Now what was Anna's married name? Gollaux, Gabeau—no, it wasn't either. It was Gavino. She leafed through the pages. There were several people of that name, but only one of them was listed as an architect, and she dialled the number, hoping that Anna was home.

The warm voice of her friend reassured her that she was, and happily Robyn made arrangements to drive over and see her that very day.

'I'll try and get to you by lunchtime,' she promised. 'But the roads might be crowded, so don't worry if I'm late.'

Then it was upstairs to change into one of her pretty new dresses, a silky voile in misty blues and lilacs, with a wide-brimmed sunhat to match. Definitely Ascot, she solemnly told her reflection before going downstairs again.

She was crossing the hall when the telephone rang. She was standing right beside it and she picked it up. It was a man asking to speak to Mr Dexter.

'He's in Rome,' she said. 'May I help you? I'm his secretary.'

'Then what does that make me?' came the amused reply. 'I thought I was.'

Robyn was startled. This was the unknown Martin, the shadowy man who had worked for Brad for ten years. His voice sounded nice, and she wondered how old he was. Probably in his early fifties; young enough for Bradley not to regard him as a father figure, but old enough not to be competitive. As if competition would ever worry Bradley Dexter! That man would have women floating around him when he was ninety!

'Is there anything I can do?' she asked, remembering she was on the telephone.

'Brad promised to let me have some books,' came the answer. 'I'm going out of my mind with boredom, stuck here.'

'If you can tell me the books you want, and give me your address, I'll bring them over to you.'

'I live in Antibes,' he said. 'I have a little house on the ramparts. But please don't bother. Perhaps Kim could deliver them to me later on.'

'I'll be quite happy to do it,' said Robyn, curious to meet him. 'Expect me in half an hour.'

She hurried away to find the books he had requested—a batch of fairly recent best-sellers which she found on one of the shelves at the far end of the living room—the area where Brad was supposed to write, but didn't. It was certainly a far more luxurious study than the room in which he really did his work, being decorated in the best Italian modern style, with furniture as seen in a Zarach showroom, and John Siddeley touches in the elegant curtains and velvet-covered banquettes that ran the length of two walls. It was interesting that Brad should keep his study proper away from prying eyes, and she wondered if he did the same with his innermost emotions: hiding the real ones and only letting you see the carefully formulated and maintained ones. It was an intriguing idea, but she had no time to speculate on it, and with the books under her arm she went out to the car.

As she bowled down the drive, her spirits were high as befitted the cloudless blue sky and the golden sunshine. A refreshing breeze half-lifted her hat and she took it off and slung it on to the back seat.

The gates at the end of the drive were closed, but as she approached them they opened automatically, snugly closing behind her as she drove through.

There was little traffic on the Cap, though it increased as she descended the hill towards Antibes. On her right the blue sea lapped into the bay, and ahead of her she glimpsed the rampart walls as they wound around the rocks and out of sight.

Glad she had thought to bring a map with her, she drew into the kerb and studied it, then set off confidently for the ramparts. She was somewhat put out to find it was only possible to drive one way down the winding road set into the wall, for it meant her going into the old part of the town to bring her to the beginning of the road. But eventually she managed to find her way through the maze of narrow streets—it was still early enough for the market to be in full swing, which did not make her task any easier—and she set off along the ramparts in search of Martin's house.

It was certainly a lovely spot in which to live, she mused, slowing the car to admire the view. Below the thick walls the sea foamed gently upon the rocks, and further out, boats bobbed upon the water, the waves scintillating like faceted glass.

Most of the houses were tall and narrow and joined to their neighbours on both sides. Some of them were newly painted, though several had been gutted and were being completely rebuilt. But they still exuded an overall impression of antiquity; as if they had been standing here casting shuttered eyes upon the Crusader boats as they set sail for the Holy Land.

The house she was looking for stood on its own and was larger than the rest. It was painted white and had dark blue shutters, which matched the dark blue door. The roof was flat, and glancing up Robyn glimpsed a roof terrace and blue and white awning. The place did not look as if it was let into flatlets, but had the aura of belonging to one person, which meant Martin either had a private income or was an exceptionally well-paid secretary. With some curiosity Robyn rang the bell.

A middle-aged woman in a dark print dress opened the door almost at once and, as if expecting her visitor, indicated for Robyn to climb the stairs.

'*Tout droit, tout droit,*' she intoned, and Robyn climbed to the top and entered a delightful studio room, with cream-tiled floor, pale green walls and white bamboo furniture with gaily covered cushions. Sliding glass doors opened on to the patio she had seen from down below, which was aflame with flowers.

But it was the man in the room who caught her attention, and she was unable to hide her surprise, for he was Bradley Dexter's age. Though not as macho in appearance, he was none the less tall, slim and attractive, with sandy brown hair and warm brown eyes.

'Hullo, Robyn Barrett,' he smiled, standing up to greet her.

She saw that his right arm was in a sling and that plaster covered it from wrist to elbow.

He saw her eyes on it and smiled: 'That's the reason *you're* here! But now you are, I hope you'll take pity on me and keep me company for a while.'

'Only for a little while,' she smiled, sitting down. 'I'm on my way to Monte Carlo.'

They eyed one another, both obviously liking what they saw.

'Brad wasn't expecting a woman,' said Martin. 'But I suppose you know that?'

'He left me in no doubt!'

He chuckled, and Robyn searched for something to say. She was not sure if Brad had told him the sort of girl he had found her to be, and she hoped he would give her a clue as he went on speaking.

'Brad's very pleased with you,' the man said. 'He told me you're very bright, and capable—for a woman.'

'He's pretty bright and capable for a man!' She looked around the room and then through the window. 'You have a wonderful view. I'd never get tired of looking at it.'

'It's even nicer in the winter when the sea's rough and the waves wash over the walls. In summer there are too many cars and the tourists spoil it.'

'But you don't live here all the year round, do you?'

'No. But I come back here pretty often. Brad looks on the villa as his home base.'

'I'd rather expected you to live with him,' Robyn admitted.

'Never,' he said emphatically. 'Fond though I am of him, I like to have my own pad where I can relax.'

'It's a beautiful pad,' she enthused.

'It wasn't always. When I bought the house five years ago it was a ruin, but I've renovated it bit by bit.' He stood up and went over to a cupboard. 'What can I offer you to drink?'

'Something long and cool, then I must be going.'

'Not permanently, I hope. I'd like to see you again if you'd care to come out with me one evening. I can't drive, but we're within walking distance of a good restaurant. Or we could eat here. Madame Vernier is an excellent cook.'

'I'd like to see you again,' Robyn said frankly. 'And I don't care where we go.' She stood up and went over to him, watching as he deftly squeezed an orange into a tall glass with his left hand, and topped it up with Perrier water.

'I bet you work miracles when you've got both hands available!' she teased.

'I hope you'll be here to find out!' Martin saw her look away quickly. 'I didn't mean that the way it sounded,' he apologised.

She turned back to him. 'I'm glad. For a minute I wondered if you were like——' Remembering this man worked for Bradley Dexter for ten years, she did not go on, but he seemed not to mind her tactlessness and gave her a rueful glance as he sat down.

'I'm the exact opposite to Brad, I'm afraid—a dull stick and never the life of the party. But it's because we're opposites that we get on so well.'

Robyn was curious to know how they had met, but did not think it politic to question him, so she finished her drink quickly and rose to leave, promising to see him for dinner in two days' time.

It was shortly after one when she arrived at Anna's flat,

an airy spacious one in a large block on the upper heights of Monte Carlo, and giving a glimpse of the fairytale palace of the Grimaldi family.

'When are you going to meet *your* prince?' Anna asked her as they sat sipping coffee on the terrace after a delicious lunch.

'Who knows?' Robyn shrugged.

'I take it you haven't met him already?' Anna teased, her greeny-brown eyes full of laughter.

Bradley Dexter's eyes, Robyn thought, and a complete image of him appeared in front of her, so real that she felt she could put out her hand and touch him. She blinked quickly and the image faded.

'No, I haven't met him yet,' she said firmly. 'I'm too involved with Hamish and Alex.'

'Who?' Anna was startled. 'Didn't your mother have a couple of Scotties by that name?'

'Exactly,' Robyn said, and started to giggle. 'But Bradley Dexter . . .'

Punctuated by gales of laughter, Robyn told her friend the whole story of her arrival at the villa and the deception she was playing on its owner. She left nothing out, and Anna was suitably indignant, though exploding with amusement at the way he had jumped out of bed naked, causing Robyn to scuttle away like a frightened crab.

'What's going to happen when he finds out you've been putting on an act?' Anna asked when the whole story had reached its end.

'Why should he find out?' Robyn asked. 'I'll never see him again once I go home.'

'Is he as good-looking as his pictures?'

'Better—and far more intelligent than his books.'

'I think his books are amusing,' Anna defended surprisingly. 'Pierre buys every new one.'

'I don't think Bradley wrote the first one to be amusing,' said Robyn. 'I believe he wrote it out of bitterness. The fact that it turned out to be funny was a bonus for him. But each new book he writes helps to keep the wound open.'

'That's a profound assertion,' Anna commented. 'And if I may be equally profound, I'd say you're falling for him.'

'I'd as soon fall for the devil,' Robyn asserted. 'Loving Bradley Dexter would be hell.' Firmly she changed the conversation. 'But you look as if you're living in heaven.'

'I am,' Anna confided. 'Pierre's wonderful. I suppose that's why I'd like to see all my friends married—I can't bear to see them single and miserable!'

Robyn laughed, but could understand what Anna meant when Pierre came home later that evening. He was even nicer than she had remembered from their wedding. Marriage had softened him and it was quite obvious he was extremely happy and doted on his wife.

He took them both to supper, to a family-run Italian restaurant which made its own pasta and the most delicious crême caramel Robyn had ever tasted.

'I don't see why you have to go back to the villa tonight,' Anna stated as they sipped their after-dinner coffee. 'If Bradley Dexter's in Rome he can't object to your staying the night with us. Do say yes, Robyn, I've a spare room that hardly anyone ever uses.'

'Except me, when Anna and I quarrel,' Pierre joked.

'Once in three years,' his wife pouted.

'And then only for half the night,' he agreed, catching hold of her hand and bringing it to his lips.

Anna ignored the gesture and went on looking at Robyn. 'Do stay,' she pleaded. 'Then I'll show you around the shops in the morning and you can leave after lunch.'

Robyn gave in, finding it decidedly pleasant to be among friends and able to behave in her normal manner. It was amazing what a strain it was to maintain her act with Brad.

'I'd better phone the villa to tell Kim not to expect me home tonight.' She went to rise, but Pierre restrained her.

'I'll do it for you, if you give me the number.'

She did so and he went away, returning a few minutes later, smiling.

'No problem,' he said. 'Mr Dexter was home and I spoke to him personally.'

'Oh, lord!' Robyn was discomfited. 'I'd better leave very early in the morning. He may want to start work at nine.'

'He doesn't,' Pierre informed her. 'I asked if he wanted you back at a special time, and he said no.'

Although Robyn professed to believe it, she was uneasy, and the next morning, resisting Anna's blandishments to show her the lovely shops—'Anyway, I couldn't afford to buy anything at Monaco prices,' Robyn stoutly averred— she set off at a brisk speed for Cap d'Antibes.

Even so it was after ten-thirty when she reached the villa, and parking the Fiat next to the scarlet Ferrari— how like Bradley Dexter it looked, with its lean aggressive lines—she ran up to her room to change. As she reached the corridor, Brad came towards her, bare feet padding on the marble floor, striped denim shorts low on his hips.

'You're a fast worker,' he drawled, his American accent normally slight, much stronger now.

'In what way?' she asked.

'For a girl who said she didn't know anyone down here, you aren't doing too badly. I take it Monsieur Gabino is a Frenchman?'

'Yes, a very charming one, as it so happens.'

'I gathered that you thought so. When he discovered he was speaking to your employer, he said he hoped I wouldn't mind if you spent the night with him.'

Robyn remembered Pierre's habit of getting his pronouns muddled and guessed Anna's husband had said 'him' when he meant 'us'. But it was a fortuitous mistake, for it established her character once and for all in Brad's eyes.

'I'll be ready to start work with you in ten minutes,' she said coolly. 'In the study or by the pool?'

'In the study, and make it five minutes.'

Almost as if to punish her—though why she was not sure—Brad dictated without stopping for most of the day, and it was six o'clock when he finally went up the spiral staircase leading to his bedroom.

Robyn's wrist was aching, and she let the pencil clatter to the desk. 'Will you want me to type this back tomorrow,' she asked, 'or will you want to continue with the dictation?'

'I'll carry on with you—workwise, I mean—as long as the muse lasts.' As he reached the door of his bedroom, he paused. 'I'll say goodnight, Robyn. I'll see you at nine in the morning.'

That evening Robyn dined with Kim and his wife, resolutely refusing to think where Bradley Dexter was, or with whom. She wondered about Martin, and what made him content to live his life in the shadow of such a scintillating employer. Few girls would give him a second look when Bradley Dexter was around, though perhaps he was satisfied to be second choice. Somehow she could not imagine it, for there was a resolution about his demeanour that spoke of character. It would be nice to go out with him tomorrow night, and at least it would stop her focusing her attention on Brad.

She pondered on what to wear, and later, upstairs in her room, picked out the dress, knowing that if Bradley worked her as hard tomorrow as he had done today, she would have little time left over for doing so.

She was not asleep when she heard him come home, though it was well into the early hours of the morning. His step was firm in the corridor outside her room and he

closed his door quietly. Whoever had had the benefit of
him tonight had had a sober lover.

Sharp at nine the next morning Robyn was in the study
ready to start work. At one minute past nine Bradley
Dexter came down the spiral staircase from his bedroom,
clad in a short terry towelling robe, loosely tied around
the waist. He flung himself down in the black leather chair
and stared at her.

Robyn stared back at him, itemising him as he had
once done with her. Glinting eyes, very green, which suggested temper; curving dark eyebrows drawn together
above his straight nose, and well-shaped mouth, which at
the moment was set in a tight line of disapproval. He was
every inch bad-tempered male, and she knew she had
done something to cause it. Triumph and fear coursed
through her, but she showed neither.

'Why didn't you tell me you'd met Martin?' he
demanded.

So that was it. 'It slipped my mind,' she said cau-
tiously.

'How the hell could it?'

'I don't know, but it did. I had no reason to hide it
from you. I never even gave it a thought.'

'Well, he's given *you* plenty of thought! I suppose you
know you've bowled him over?'

Robyn was too aware of her looks not to guess this
might have happened.

'I thought he was rather nice too,' she said placatingly.

'He is nice—too damn nice for you to play around
with.'

'What makes you think I'm playing?'

'Well, aren't you?' Not waiting for her to reply, he went
on angrily, 'You're to leave Martin alone. He's had
enough trouble in his life without falling for a girl like
you.'

'What's wrong with me? I don't do anything you

wouldn't do. Or are you going to be old-fashioned and say it's different for a woman?'

'I happen to think it *is* different for a woman. You may look like an angel, but you're anything but,' he snapped. 'A few more years of loose living and it will start to show on your face.'

'It doesn't show on yours,' she said brightly. 'You look quite rested today, though I'm sure you had a very active night.'

'We're discussing you, not me, and I meant what I said before. I don't want you to see Martin.'

'You can't tell me what to do in my free time.'

He scowled and jumped up. His towelling jacket loosened and she quickly averted her eyes, hiding her relief when he belted it tightly.

'I'd like to tell you a story, Robyn,' he went on. The temper had gone from his voice and it was his normally deep attractive one. 'I've known Martin since we were kids together at boarding school. I lost touch with him when I ran away and only met up with him when I was writing my first book. He was twenty-four, the same age as me, and married to a pretty girl called Elizabeth. I've never seen a guy so happy—until the day she ran off with her skiing instructor in Aspen. It damn near broke him, and if I hadn't helped to pull him out of it, he'd now be a drunken wreck. It's only in the last few years that he's become his old self again, and the one thing I don't want to happen is for him to fall for a girl like you.'

'Thanks,' she said sarcastically. 'You're full of compliments.'

'I'm being honest with you. That's a compliment in itself.' He sat down and stretched his muscular legs out on the stool in front of him. 'You're a beautiful girl, Robyn, but you've got no heart, which is why I don't want you breaking Martin's. You're promiscuous and you're not interested in marriage, so on all counts you aren't what he's looking for.'

'Don't you think Martin's old enough to decide that for himself?'

'Not where you're concerned. You look too much like his ex-wife, and since he's still in love with her . . .'

Robyn was disconcerted by the answer, but not for long.

'It might do Martin good to fall in love with me and find out what a dreadful girl I am,' she said brightly. 'The shock might make him decide to look for someone who isn't like his ex-wife.'

'Or he might fall even harder for you than he did for Elizabeth. You're twice the girl she was.'

Unaccountably Robyn was pleased. 'You mean I'm prettier?'

Brad turned his head, his cheek rested on the black leather back of his chair, which outlined the firmness of the bone structure. Definitely not a man to play with, she thought inconsequentially.

'You're beautiful,' he said softly, 'but deadly. So be a good girl and leave Martin alone.' Not waiting for her answer, but seemingly taking it for granted she would do as he said, he motioned that he was ready to start work.

This day was a repetition of the previous one, though it was interrupted by a call from Holly, whom he dismissed with cruel speed.

'On with the new?' Robyn asked flippantly when he had put the phone down on the girl.

'That's my motto,' he flipped back. 'Love 'em and leave 'em. Or perhaps I should say, lust 'em and leave 'em.' He eyed her, and chuckled. 'How do you manage to do it, Robyn?'

'Do it?' she repeated, not sure what he meant.

'Blush,' he explained. 'How do you manage to go so fascinatingly pink of cheek when you're about as innocent as the devil?'

'It's a little trick I learned,' she said demurely, and held her pencil poised above her notepad to show she was ready to resume work.

As on the previous evening he stopped at six, wished her goodnight, and went to his room to change. Robyn did the same, but was careful to stay in her own room until she heard him drive away. Only then did she set off to meet Martin.

Knowing about his past made her see him with different eyes, and for the first few moments with him she was terribly selfconscious. But he was an easy conversationalist, and during dinner, which they had in an airy, flower-filled restaurant on the Cap road, she relaxed and became her normal self. She made Martin laugh as she told him about some of the strange authors she had met during the two years she had worked at Morton Publishing, and this led them to talk about books in general and plays in particular. They found out they were both avid theatregoers, which, he confessed, was something he missed while living down here.

'I spend two weeks in New York at the beginning of spring and the beginning of winter, seeing every new play,' he admitted. 'But it's not the same as being able to go when the fancy takes you.' His hand moved across the table and lightly touched her pink-tipped one. 'My fancy has taken me very much in your direction, Robyn,' he said softly.

'Because I look like your ex-wife?'

His hand drew back and he sat rigid with shock. 'Brad,' he said flatly. 'I suppose he told you the whole story?'

'Only to warn me not to hurt you,' she confessed, not wanting him to think badly of a man who cared so deeply for his friend. 'He doesn't believe I'm the right girl for you, and I think he's right,' she added, realising that charming though Martin was, there was no special zing between them.

'Don't decide so quickly,' Martin replied. 'I still want to see you again—if you'll let me.'

'Why not try a redhead?' Robyn suggested, 'and give blondes a miss for a while?'

'I'm no longer in love with Elizabeth,' he answered. 'But Brad won't believe it. He still insists I haven't got her out of my system.'

'Because he equates you with himself. Brad's never forgotten his own anguish, so he can't believe you'll ever forget yours.'

Martin gave a slight smile and shake of his head. 'You've got it wrong, I'm afraid. Brad's never anguished over a girl as long as I've known him. And he never will, either.'

'I wasn't talking about a girl. I was referring to the way he feels about his mother.'

Martin's eyes widened, then moved over her face as if trying to read her mind.

'How do you know about his mother?'

'He told me. Not the whole story, but most of it. About not being wanted, and being left in school for most of his young years.'

'I've never known him admit that story to anyone,' Martin said incredulously. 'Maggie and I are the only two people who know how deeply it affected him.'

'Who's Maggie?' Robyn asked, her heart giving an uncomfortable thump in her chest.

'His aunt—the one he went to see in Rome.'

'So it was true!' Robyn was inexplicably delighted, and it showed on her face.

'Didn't you believe him?' Martin questioned. 'He admires his aunt more than anyone else he knows. When his own parents were traipsing all over the world, she wanted him to live with her. But his mother wouldn't hear of it. There was no love lost between the two sisters-in-law, and she even forbade Maggie to go and see him when he was at school. Not that Maggie took any notice of her. She'd come down two or three times each term, and during the school holidays when there was only one teacher left to watch over him. If it hadn't been for his aunt, Brad would have run away from school when he was fourteen, but she persuaded him to stick it out a bit longer.'

'I'm glad to hear there's *one* woman in the world he doesn't despise,' Robyn said on a sigh.

'There are quite a few women he doesn't despise,' Martin responded. 'Don't be fooled by what he says. The only trouble is that the moment he meets a nice girl— someone who's sweet and honest and could genuinely love him—he runs a mile. He'll never let himself fall in love,' he went on. 'Never.'

It was interesting to know Bradley Dexter's cynicism of the female race was a pose. However it would not change his life-style, and his future was likely to be as untouched by genuine warmth as his past. Poor Brad!

Robyn blinked her eyes as the man occupying her mind walked across the well-lit room towards their table.

In a pale grey safari suit, sleeves rolled back to disclose muscular arms, and a darker grey silk shirt open at the throat, he was so preposterously good-looking that Robyn caught her breath. How fast would he run away from the real me? she wondered, and knew that had she been aware of Bradley Dexter's past when they had first met, she would never have embarked on this ridiculous act.

Yet as his eyes glinted down at her she revised her opinion. It was pure conceit on her part to think that with her, he might have been different. Bradley Dexter would never change. Lust for 'em and then leave 'em. That was the axiom by which he lived, and she must never allow herself to forget it.

'I didn't know you were dining here,' said Martin. 'Come and join us.'

'Only for a drink,' Brad replied. 'Marcia doesn't like to share me.'

A tall, soignée-looking brunette undulated towards them. Her casual white pleated dress was not a copy of the Dior one Robyn had seen on the front page of this month's *Vogue*, but the couture one itself; as real as the sapphire and gold necklace around her throat, each blue stone half an inch in size. An even larger sapphire weighed down her left hand, not quite masking a diamond wedding ring.

'Lovely to see you, Marcia,' said Martin, standing to kiss her.

'Darling!' she cooed, too busy eyeing Robyn to return the compliment.

'My temporary secretary,' Brad murmured casually. 'Shall we join them for a drink before we go to our table?'

'Anything you say, darling.'

Ignoring Robyn, Marcia commandeered the conversation, and Bradley let her, smiling at her jokes, which were quite witty, and sipping the inevitable glass of champagne.

Sourly Robyn watched him, wondering if he knew he was by far the best-looking man in the room, and deciding that he did.

'We're going on to the Casino after dinner,' he suddenly announced. 'What about you two joining us?'

Robyn met Martin's eyes. She knew he was happy to do whatever she wished and, frightened by the strange feelings Brad was arousing in her, feelings she wanted to deny even though she refused to admit them, she shook her head.

'I'd rather sit on your lovely roof terrace and listen to music.'

'There's your answer, Brad,' said Martin, looking so pleased that Robyn immediately regretted her decision. No matter what she felt towards Bradley Dexter, she had no intention of hurting his friend.

'I think we're de trop,' Marcia said, pulling Brad to his feet. 'You'll have to make do with me.'

I'll bet he's already made do with you, Robyn thought bitchily and, as Brad turned away and their eyes met, the sudden thrust of his jaw told her he had guessed her thoughts.

'Pretty girl,' Robyn murmured when she and Martin were alone. 'Where's the husband?'

'Divorced, along with husband number one. She's hoping to be third time lucky with Brad.'

'How stupid can you get?'

'That's what Brad says,' Martin grinned. 'But she's a stunner, isn't she?'

'A stunner,' Robyn echoed, and took a sip of wine, which suddenly seemed to taste bitter.

Later, in Martin's house, they sat on the roof terrace and did listen to music. But it was not as romantic as she had hoped, nor was she in the mood to be kissed.

'Just friends,' she said firmly when Martin made a second attempt to draw her into his arms, and though he looked faintly surprised, he accepted the rebuff.

She was pretty sure Brad had told him the sort of girl he thought her to be, and though she wished she could tell him it was a lie, she knew it was dangerous to do so. Martin was Brad's friend, as well as secretary, and he would never allow him to be played for a fool. It required no imagination to guess how furious Brad would be when he discovered the trick she had played on him—especially if he learned it from someone else—and there and then she made up her mind that at the very first opportunity she would tell him the truth about herself. If it made him see her as fair game, and she found she couldn't hold him off, she would return to London. Yet somehow she had the conviction that he would not make a pass at her. In the two weeks she had been at the villa, an empathy had developed between them that would make him treat her as an equal and not as a plaything.

'Why so pensive?' Martin asked.

It was on the tip of her tongue to tell him, but she held back, knowing she had to talk to Brad first. Only then would she be free to be herself.

CHAPTER SIX

WHEN Robyn drove into the garage, she was surprised to find Brad's Ferrari already there. It was only one o'clock and she had not expected him to leave the lovely Marcia's side so early—especially as they were going to the Casino—unless he had brought her home with him. It was an unpleasant thought, and she tossed her head, angry that it should be.

Dropping the key of the car on the hall table, she went up the stairs, her fingers trailing on the bronze handrail. It was a lovely staircase, as indeed it was a lovely villa— apart from the dreadful modern paintings. With the removal of these, and some feminine touches in the downstairs rooms, the villa would make an ideal permanent home. Not that Bradley Dexter wanted anything permanent.

As she turned at the top of the stairs to walk down the corridor to her room, she saw him standing at the far end watching her. Her heart seemed to skip a beat and then to pound furiously. Suddenly nervous of him, yet not knowing why, for his anger did not matter to her, she walked slowly towards her bedroom.

'I want to talk to you, Robyn.'

It was useless pretending she had not heard him. 'Couldn't it wait until the morning?' she asked. 'I'm tired.'

'It won't take long.' He swung open the door of his study and she had no option but to walk past her bedroom and join him.

Although she had determined to tell him the truth about herself, one look at his set expression warned her that now was not the time. He was too furious to see the funny side of it, and would either send her packing immediately—without the manuscript—or possibly not even believe she was telling him the truth. From the glitter in his eyes as they swept over her, she knew with a sinking heart that he was far more likely to see her confession as yet another trick. She would have to wait until tomorrow, when he was in a better mood.

He was in a fine temper. It was apparent in the set of his shoulder and mouth, and the virulent look he gave her as he took in her hair, which was dishevelled from the breeze that had blown in from the open window as she had driven home, but which, as his next words showed, he assumed to be from a different reason.

'I thought I told you to leave Martin alone?' he demanded.

'And I thought I told you that what I did in my free time was my own affair!'

'Since it's only an affair you're looking for, won't I do?'

Her heart began to beat even faster. 'No, you won't.'

'That isn't the message I've sometimes read in your eyes.'

'Then you've misread it,' she snapped, and went to turn away from him. 'I prefer my men to be less obvious.'

'That's the way I prefer my women,' he said, coming towards her and pulling her back against him. 'But since you're alone and I'm alone——'

'Where's Marcia?'

'I left her at the Casino. She wanted to go on playing and I didn't.'

'Then don't come home to play with me!'

Robyn tried to pull free of him, and knew instantly that it was the worst thing she could have done, for his grip tightened and he pressed her body back against his. She felt the hardness of his frame down the length of her spine, and the steely strength of his thighs pressing against her buttocks.

'That's exactly what I've come home to do,' he said thickly. 'It's what I've wanted from the minute I saw you walking across the side of the pool towards me, your beautiful face full of disdain.'

'My beautiful face is still full of disdain,' she grated, forcing herself to remain inert against him in the hope that he would let her go.

'That isn't what your heart's saying.' His breath tickled her ear. 'It's pounding like a trapped bird's. But it can't be from fear, can it, my little Robyn—or shall I call you my little cuckoo, for *they* don't mind which nest they lie in either, do they?'

'*I* happen to mind very much,' she snapped. 'And I don't want to stay in yours, Bradley Dexter.'

'I'm sure I can make you change your mind.'

His arms moved swiftly, one of them cupping her shoulders and the other gripping her under the knees as he swung her up into his arms and purposefully mounted the stairs to his bedroom.

'Let me go!' she cried fearfully, pounding his chest. 'What do you think you're doing?'

'I'll give you three guesses!'

'Put me down!' she cried again. 'Put me down!'

For answer he dropped her on to the centre of the bed, at the same time placing his body on top of hers. Although he supported himself with his elbows, his weight prevented her from struggling; nor could she lever her knees to try to kick him, for his legs were like iron bars upon her own.

'Why pretend you don't want me?' he whispered. 'We've been wanting each other from the beginning. Stop playing coy with me, Robyn.'

One of his hands came up to catch hold of her face, but as he bent to her mouth she twisted her head sideways and his lips came to rest on her throat. He gave a triumphant laugh and moved them swiftly down to the curve of her shoulder, then lower still, to where the creamy mound of her breasts could be glimpsed through the low neckline of her dress.

A tremor went through Robyn and he felt it. 'You see,' he whispered exultantly. 'You do want me!'

With the ease of long practice his hands were behind her, adroitly unzipping her dress. Even as she continued to struggle, she realised the futility of it, for the silky bodice slipped from her and his eyes blazed down upon tiptilted breasts whose pink nipples resembled the tiny tea-roses that clustered round the narrow pillars along the terrace.

If only I'd worn a bra, Robyn thought despairingly, but knew that even this would have been no barrier, for Brad's lips had curved themselves upon her softness, and he was using tongue and teeth to arouse her to an ecstasy of desire she had never before experienced.

'You're beautiful,' he said thickly. 'Every part of you. Don't fight me, sweetheart. We were meant for each other.'

His hands moved with surprising gentleness around her waist and along the soft swell of her stomach, then down over the curve of her hips, removing her dress at the same time. It was so skilfully done that Robyn found herself naked except for her brief silk panties. As the tips of his fingers softly eased their way into them, she knew she had reached crisis point in her relationship with him.

If she had been able to confess the truth about herself before he had brought her into his bedroom, she might have stood a chance of making him believe her. But if she did it now, he would think she was putting on yet another act. By the time he discovered that she wasn't, it would be too late, because he would already have taken her.

The jerkiness of his movements made it clear he was not going to wait long before doing so, and the waves of desire he was arousing in her by his sensual touch told her she was not capable of putting up too much of a fight. But she had to fight. It was more than a determination to retain her virginity; it was the knowledge that once she had given in to him she would want to go on giving. And he was not a man who would want to go on taking—at least not from the same woman.

With a cunning born of desperation she saw there was only one way to play this scene: and that was with the same ice-cold logic which she had so far successfully used to keep him at bay.

'Relax, darling,' he whispered. 'Let me hold you without having to fight you.'

Instantly she lay passive. 'I'm not fighting you, Brad,' she said, making her voice as husky as she could. 'I'm fighting myself.'

'Why bother?' His tongue trailed warm fire across her stomach. 'We both know you're going to give in.'

'Of course I am, but not for twenty-five minutes.'

His tongue stilled its movement. 'What did you say?'

'Not for twenty-five minutes. It's most important for me to be aroused properly, and it always takes me that long.'

'I'd say you were pretty aroused already.'

'That's what you think.' Wickedly she sank her teeth into his shoulder.

'Hey!' He jerked upwards. 'That hurt!'

'I'm terrible when I'm really aroused,' she said, nibbling the bronze skin like a bee imbibing pollen. 'Don't rush me, Brad. You'll miss out on a lot of fun if you do. Play it slowly, and put on all the lights.'

'What?' He was startled.

'I want to see you properly. That way, I won't confuse you with anyone else. Put on the lights,' she insisted.

'Not all of them,' he protested, reaching out to touch a switch on the headboard, which illumined several soft lamps on the far wall.

Following his hand, Robyn pressed all the switches she could, and every single light in the room flashed on, as well as the soft strains of a Cole Porter melody, while from a hidden cupboard on the left of her a little gold trolley glided into view, bearing an ice bucket and a bottle of champagne.

Robyn gaped at it, and all at once was struck by the humour of the situation. She tried to stifle her laughter, but it was impossible. It burst out of her and she collapsed upon the pillow in a paroxysm of mirth.

'How predictable you are! I expected soft lights and sweet music, but I thought even *you* would draw the line at automated trolleys with champagne on them! What happens next?' Her laughter intensified. 'Does the bed start vibrating?'

Hardly had she spoken, when it did, and she gave another scream of mirth.

'Oh no! You're not only predictable, Bradley Dexter, you're positively old-fashioned. I can't believe it!'

'Well, believe this,' he muttered in a fury, and lifting himself away from her, every bronze muscle quivering with rage, he picked her up, strode across the room and deposited her outside the door. 'I'm sure you won't find *this* so predictable!' he snapped, and banged the door shut in her face.

Robyn fled to her room.

Only in its safety did the tears come, washing away the laughter and making her accept the unpleasant, unbelievable truth. She had fallen in love with a man she despised.

Far into the night she kept trying to deny it, using every excuse to make herself believe that what she was experiencing was a shallow and purely physical emotion. But she knew it was more than that. Of course part of it was physical—she would be lying if she said it weren't—but it was cerebral too. Brad's wicked sense of humour, his sharp mind and the tough way he had built his life afresh, aroused her admiration even though she disliked many of the things he had done. But she could find an excuse for every one of his unpleasant actions; could find valid reasons why he should be faithless, despise women, use them as playthings. And each excuse she made for him brought it home to her how deeply he had burrowed his way into her heart.

But she was not too far gone to know there was no future in loving him. All too clearly she saw the hopelessness of it. Bradley desired her very much and, more important still, he had a reluctant respect for her intelligence. She knew he rarely experienced this in a woman, which was probably one reason why he had not tried to make love to her before. But if he realised she genuinely cared for him, he would immediately send her away.

So where did that leave her? Common sense told her to return to London at once, but two things stopped her. Not only loyalty to Morton Phillips, but her own pride, which made it imperative that Brad should never guess how she felt. Painful though it was going to be, she must stay here till the book was completed.

It was a dispirited girl who made her way down to breakfast the following morning, head aching after a sleepless night. To hide her shadowed eyes she wore dark glasses, and to keep her lank hair away from her face— fatigue always made it lose some of its bounce—she had confined it in a scarlet snood that matched her scarlet shirtwaister.

So it was that Brad found her at the breakfast table, her outward appearance bright, provocative, and infinitely sophisticated.

'Playing Miss Garbo?' he asked sourly, gulping down his orange juice.

'Not playing at all.'

'Nor am I.' He sat down and reached for a croissant.

Fascinated, Robyn watched him spread it thickly with butter and a dollop of jam.

'I thought you never ate breakfast,' she asked faintly.

'I've turned over a new leaf.'

'What did you find under it?' she asked.

'A beautiful crab-apple.' One croissant went down and he reached for another. 'I suppose it's no good asking you not to see Martin?'

'That's right.' She sipped her coffee.

'And it's equally no good suggesting you make do with me?'

'I gave you my answer to that last night.'

'Then the only way I can stop you from doing any harm is to keep you a hundred per cent occupied, a hundred per cent of the time.'

'Not in your arms!' she flared.

'At the typewriter,' he retorted, and glanced at the narrow sliver of gold on his wrist. 'I'll see you in twenty minutes in the study. We've some long hard days ahead of us, Robyn, and you'll have no chance to fly to anyone's nest.'

He was as bad as his word and, for the rest of the week, worked almost without cessation. Though he stopped promptly at six each night, remembering her earlier assertion that she only worked overtime in an emergency, she was so exhausted by then that she was too tired to accept any of Martin's invitations to dinner. But Brad was inexhaustible and would disappear each evening, not returning until the early hours of the morning. But always alone.

Robyn found herself trembling each time she heard his car screech to a halt in the garage, and she would wait expectantly for the sound of two voices. But they never came, and she would snuggle back down in her bed, content yet ashamed that she should feel this way about a man whose whole life was totally opposed to her own.

On Thursday evening she was alone as usual in the living room, dinner over, and listening to music, when Martin walked in.

'If the mountain won't come to Mahomet . . .' he said by way of a greeting, and kissed the silvery blonde top of her hair.

When she made a move to rise, he pushed her gently back against the cushions. 'Relax, Robyn.' He seated himself opposite her. 'You look beautiful, but tired. I take it demon work is to blame?'

She sighed. 'How long can he go on at such a pace?'

'I've never known him flag yet. It's up to you to tell him if you want to ease up. You're not a machine, you know.'

'Brad thinks I am.'

'I'm glad to hear it,' Martin smiled. 'Till now he's always had first chance with the girls without any fight from me. But you're different. You know that, don't you?'

Robyn was silent and Martin inched his chair forward. 'I could very easily fall for you,' he went on. 'I don't suppose you'd consider giving up your job and moving in with me, with a view to matrimony?'

'How long a view?'

'Three weeks. It would take that long to get a licence!'

She laughed and shook her head. 'I appreciate the offer, but it's no go. We hardly know each other.'

'Then let's get acquainted.'

'I can't spare the time. If Brad goes on at this rate, I'll be in London in a fortnight with the book.'

'Will you see me if I come to London?'

'Why not?' She closed her eyes and let the music drift over her. Neither of them bothered to make conversation, except when Martin rose to put on a new tape. The sky darkened to navy blue and frogs croaked in a distant pool on the estate.

It was in the spirit of companionable togetherness that Brad walked in and found them.

'Am I intruding?' he asked, firmly turning on the lights.

'Unfortunately not,' Martin replied, and rose to leave.

Robyn guessed that his years of friendship had attuned him as to how far he could go with Brad whose hazel eyes had become like chips of ice, though he was still smiling.

'You shouldn't be driving,' said Brad, moving to the door with him.

'I'm not. I came in a taxi.'

'I'll drive you back, then.'

The two men went out, and the instant Robyn heard the roar of the Ferrari, she scuttled to her room, and locked the door. There had been a glint in Brad's eye which she distrusted, and she would give him no opportunity to get close to her again.

The next morning, she expected him to comment on Martin's appearance at the villa, but he did not refer to it. Thinking about it during the fifteen-minute break he allowed them for lunch, when she hastily swallowed a sandwich and drank a reviving cup of coffee, she realised this was typical of him. Since she had evidently shattered his ego by calling him predictable, he was now determined not to be.

He worked her at the same ferocious pace in the afternoon, and her wrist ached as she kept up the endless flow of shorthand that filled page after page. It was all excellent stuff, witty as ever, but with an even sharper sting to it than his last book, as he pointed out the pitfalls of marriage and showed how men through the ages had managed to have their cake and eat it.

As usual he stopped at six o'clock, but instead of disappearing to his room to change and go out, he paused and looked at her.

'Is this your first trip to the south of France?'

She shook her head. 'I came here once with my parents, years ago. I was about ten.'

'Then you don't know the restaurants here?'

'Only the Bacon, where Martin took me.'

'I'm going to take you somewhere far nicer. Meet me downstairs at eight.'

'Why the invitation?' she questioned, ignoring the way her pulses were racing.

'Because I've worked you like a dog and you haven't complained.'

He ran lightly up the spiral staircase, leaving her looking after him, dismayed that this kind and unexpected gesture should turn her bones to water. Like a girl on her first date, Robyn took out all her prettiest dresses and laid them on the bed, before deciding upon a filmy chiffon tunic, with a minimal bodice and shoestring straps. The dress was simple in the extreme, relying for effect on its delicate oyster colouring and the lovely shape of the body it partially clothed. There was a jacket to match which, though it covered her skin, made the gleam of flesh look even more provocative.

She was too exhausted to set her hair and she let it fall loosely around her shoulders, unaware that the style enhanced the faint air of fragility that hung around her. She knew it did not come from hard work alone, but from her deepening feelings for Brad, and she found herself counting the hours until she could put him and the villa completely behind her. But tonight was going to be a moment snatched out of time; one she would cherish for the rest of her life.

He was waiting for her in the hall as she came down the stairs, leaning negligently against the wall as he watched her. He was dressed impeccably, in beige slacks and jacket, with a deeper brown, open-necked shirt. As she came on a level with him he turned and strode out to the Ferrari parked at the foot of the steps. Silently he held the door open for her, then took his place behind the wheel.

He did not speak and Robyn forced herself to relax. It was not easy when he was so close beside her, his lean fingers moving the gear lever and occasionally, inadvertently, brushing against her thigh. But as the car greedily ate up the miles, she found a strange peace in being close to him.

The coast road gave way to the Corniche as they left Nice behind them and climbed up towards the purple sky, whose stars twinkled down on a scene of fairytale beauty. Cypress-covered hills were dotted with villas, some half hidden, some proudly displaying themselves. Far down on the coast, glittering lights marked the esplanade, with here and there a brighter flash of light indicating restaurants and hotels. It was not yet high season and the road was not too crowded, so that they were still able to make a fast pace along the winding road.

Brad controlled the car with the same ease he controlled his women. I'm the only one he hasn't managed to control, Robyn thought, and wondered how long this would be true if she continued to stay here.

They reached a fork in the road and took the right one, descending sharply down to the pretty town of Beaulieu. There were only a few people on the streets and the shops were closed, but the lights in them were on and she glimpsed beautiful antique furniture and paintings. They passed a delightful little casino which resembled an iced gâteau, and then Brad slackened speed as they reached the sandy-beige façade of a small hotel, with its own car park into which he swung.

'La Réserve.' Robyn spoke the words softly, remembering it was here that Morton Phillips had stayed after his divorce a year ago; a holiday which Robyn had declined to share with him.

'It's one of the most elegant and expensive places on the French coast,' he had told her. 'Nowhere near as ostentatious as the Hôtel de Paris in Monte Carlo, and infinitely more attractive for anyone seeking seclusion.'

Robyn knew exactly what he meant as she walked

down the flower-bordered driveway into the small lobby and thence to the pine-panelled bar. Most of the residents and visitors could be found in the large square courtyard beyond, sitting amidst more flowers and foliage, as they sipped drinks served by deft-footed waiters. The beige walls of the hotel rose on two sides of it; on the third was a fountain and on the fourth was the glass-walled restaurant, whose terrace overlooked the swimming pool and a private jetty, where motorboats could bring guests from across the bay or serve as a launching pad for water-skiers.

'Shall we have a drink first?' Brad suggested and, not waiting for her acquiescence, led her to a table. Behind them came the tinkling of a piano, playing tunes from the twenties, which seemed to go well with the ambience.

After sipping an unusual cocktail of champagne and fresh raspberry juice, Robyn followed Brad through the elegant dining room, with its floral-painted ceiling, to a table in the centre of the terrace. It was obvious he was well known here from the way the waiters buzzed around him, then discreetly left them to make their own choice of food.

But Robyn was too busy enjoying the beauty of the scene to be concerned with good eating. Entering this hotel had been like stepping back into a more gracious past, even though the man opposite her represented an extremely aggressive present and might also be destroying her future. Shying away from such an unpleasant thought, she looked at the diners. Most of them were conservatively dressed, though there were a few tables occupied by exceptionally elegant people, none of them English, she noted with some amusement. The women wore the latest fashions and had the same hard veneer as Marcia. Quite a few of them eyed Brad in the same way too, their eyes making no pretence as they devoured him. Brad seemed unaware of it, and even when she looked at him mockingly, his puzzled response showed that his unawareness was genuine.

'What's wrong now?' he asked.

'I'm just thinking how nice it is to be dining with a man whom every woman wants to eat!'

He half smiled. 'You enjoy taking an occasional bite out of me yourself, if I remember.'

'Only in self-defence,' she blushed.

'What were you defending? It couldn't have been your honour!'

'My independence. I like to have *some* say in the matter when I'm taken to bed.'

'I'll write you a little note next time, asking your permission.'

'Another ten days and I'll be gone,' she said, deciding to change the subject completely. 'The book's coming along marvellously.'

'I might not be able to keep up this pace,' he warned, 'so don't reckon on leaving quite so soon.'

She hid her surprise. Martin had told her that Brad was capable of working at this pace indefinitely, and she wondered if he intended to slow down in order to keep her here. It was an interesting thought. Brad was obviously puzzled at meeting a female who was not an immediate pushover for him, and curiosity might make him try to give her another push! Poor Brad. He would learn to his cost that she was totally unlike the women he had so far known.

'Let's call a truce for tonight,' he said abruptly. 'We've both worked hard and we're tired, so why don't we behave like two friends out together, instead of acting like cat and dog?'

'In your last book you said men and women could never be friends unless they were sexless or in their dotage.'

'We'll be the exception that disproves the rule.'

'When a man starts saying that to a woman, he's treading on dangerous ground.'

'Stop quoting me,' he growled, and rustled the menu at her.

They both chose their meal independently, somewhat surprised to find they had ordered the same thing: foie gras in brioche and baby chicken with herbes de Provence.

Relaxing in her comfortable chair, Robyn took off her jacket and let the soft sea breeze caress her skin. It was no more gentle than Brad's eyes upon her, and she was glad that the soft glow of the golden lamps that lit the terrace made it difficult for him to see her change of colour.

This was the first time she had dined with him among strangers, and she felt a strong sense of pride at knowing he outshone every man in the room. It was not only his looks—which were exceptional—but his unconscious air of style. It marked him out as someone who was used to being in a position of command. Yet there was no arrogance in the manner he displayed to the people waiting on them, and he spoke to the head waiter and the commis boys in the same easy style he displayed to his friends. No, that wasn't true either. He was far less friendly towards the men and girls she had seen at the villa than he was being here tonight. Perhaps he suited his behaviour to his surroundings: a tough, determined seducer when he was with the jet set, and a polite and charming man when among people whose lives were far removed from the exotic atmosphere that came from too much money and too much time to waste.

By the time they reached the coffee and brandy stage, Robyn was totally relaxed. She and Brad had talked like normal friends discussing other people's books rather than his own, exchanging mild gossip about writers they mutually knew, and finding they had similar tastes in a whole range of things, from enjoying walking in the rain, their liking for fried onions, and having a complete mistrust of politicians.

'Last year I was asked to stand for Parliament,' he said surprisingly.

'How can you?' She sat forward. 'You're American.'

'My father was English and I have dual nationality.'

'I can't imagine anyone taking your political aspirations seriously,' she commented.

'If'd I'd agreed to do it I'd have been very serious. But I turned it down because I happen to believe the pen is mightier than the sword.'

'Your pen would certainly make you richer,' she said, then, afraid she had sounded rude, added: 'You can always turn to politics when the ink runs dry.'

'Or when women lose their appeal for me!'

'That too,' she replied, 'although we don't have many centenarians in the Houses of Parliament!'

He laughed. 'Quick-tongued Robyn! I can see why Morton values you so highly.'

He half opened his mouth to continue and then stopped, and Robyn guessed he was curious about her relationship with his publisher. But she was glad he did not question her, though she knew it was not because he had any respect for a woman's privacy, but because he did not wish to intrude on the personal affairs of his men friends.

Dinner over, they strolled back to the car and drove slowly along the lower Corniche. They circled the harbour at Nice, which was filled mainly with fishing smacks. Most of the cafés were closed, for it was past midnight, though the Croisette was brightly lit.

Robyn wondered whether Brad was going to take her dancing or to the Casino, and was glad when he did not suggest either. She preferred to be alone with him; to have his full attention and to enjoy his unusual seriousness. He had told her a lot more about his youth. Not about his unhappy schooldays, but about the fun of his adolescence when he had roamed the world, knocking off the raw edges of his personality until he had become the polished adult of today.

Her eyes closed and she rested her head against the soft leather upholstery. How supple it was: like Brad's skin as he had rubbed his body upon her own.

When she opened her eyes again she found she was lying upon his shoulder, sprawled half way across her seat and on to his. His arm was supporting her and her hair splayed out across his jacket, looking no less silver than the moonlight. She went to straighten, nervous of his proximity, but he would not let her go and, aware of what had happened the last time she had struggled, she relaxed. For several moments he went on holding her, his grip impersonal, though the slightly increased tempo of his breathing gave away the emotions he was pretending not to have. But she felt no triumph in knowing she aroused him. How could she when nymphets like Holly and hard-faced sophisticates like Marcia could do the same? It was this thought that resolutely made her pull free of him and open the car door.

He came round the side to help her out, looming tall above her, then clasped her hand in his warm one and led her to the house. As she went towards the staircase his grip tightened and he drew her into the living room. Still holding her, as if afraid she would run away, he switched on a tape and, as the melodic strains of Nelson Riddle wafted around them, he drew her close and began to dance.

Although Robyn was a tall girl he topped her by a head, and she rested her cheek comfortably on his shoulder. Their steps matched perfectly and his body fitted into hers like a hand in a glove. She knew it would be this way if she surrendered to him, and though the thought brought pleasure, she knew she was unwilling to face the bitterness that would then follow. It was too difficult to fight against her innermost beliefs; to pretend that marriage was unimportant and that permanent commitment meant nothing. If she had fallen in love with someone who, through circumstances beyond his control, could never marry her, she would have suffered no qualms of conscience in living with him. But she was not the stuff of which casual playmates were made, and even though it would hurt her to leave Brad, she would be hurt even more if she stayed.

'Let me love you,' he whispered against her hair. 'Can't you feel how much I want you, Robyn?'

'I don't like mixing business with pleasure. I told you that when I came here.'

'Then let's make business a pleasure too. I'll dictate to you in bed!'

She chuckled and felt his body grow taut, as if he were expecting her to laugh in his face, the way she had done the other night.

'I don't find it easy to switch roles, Brad,' she said, keeping her head on his chest and refusing to look at his face, although the fast beat of his heart was almost as much her undoing. 'I came here as your temporary secretary, not your temporary girl-friend. Why do you keep persisting?'

'Why do you keep *re*sisting? We would have such fun together. You interest me far more than any girl I've known.' He stopped dancing and tilted her face up to his. 'There are hidden depths to you, Robyn, and I want to explore them. Please let me.'

His mouth came down upon hers, its touch light, and she offered no resistance. Expertly he parted her lips and began to drain the sweetness. She trembled, and he drew her down upon a settee and lay beside her, pressing her into its soft depths. Silently he went on kissing her, loving her with each sweep of his tongue, each gentle bite of his teeth, each caress of his fingers as they moved over her soft skin to rising curves and indentations, to hard nipples and soft stomach, to curving thighs and satin smooth legs. But as he went to touch the inner citadel, she pushed him away.

'No, Brad!' she said sharply. 'I won't.'

Motionless, he remained beside her. He was breathing fast and he made no effort to hide how she had aroused him.

'When we've finished the book,' he said huskily, 'tell Morton you want a holiday and then stay with me.'

'I only have another week's holiday due to me,' she said lightly, knowing that if she were not careful, she would burst into tears.

'I won't have my fill of you in a week,' he muttered. 'Why don't you leave Morton? Then you can stay here as long as you like.'

As long as *you* like, Robyn thought, and gave him a shove that sent him crashing to the floor.

Bewildered, he shook the dark hair away from his eyes and glared at her. 'What the hell did you do that for?'

'Boredom!' She stood up and marched out. 'You're becoming predictable again.'

His shout of laughter echoed in her ears as she went to her room and locked the door; though she was not sure whether it was to lock him out or to lock herself in.

CHAPTER SEVEN

MORTON PHILLIPS arrived the next afternoon, unheralded but very much welcomed by Robyn, who felt that his presence would save the situation between herself and Brad from bursting into flames.

'I had to go to Paris to see another author,' he explained as he sat beside them on a lounger by the pool, sipping a long, cool Pimms which was usually Brad's tea-time drink. 'And once I was across the Channel it seemed the natural thing to do to pop down here and see how the book was getting on.'

'We're three-quarters of the way through,' Brad replied. 'Isn't that so, Robyn?'

She nodded. Brad's behaviour to her today had been exemplary, though she had sensed that inside he was seething. Each time she had looked up from her notepad she had seen his eyes fixed on her, and occasionally he had even lost track of what he was saying, so that she had been forced to prompt him.

'When do you think it will be ready?' Morton asked.

'Two weeks,' said Robyn.

'A week,' Brad replied simultaneously, and seeing her surprise, murmured, 'I have a reason for wanting to get it out of the way.'

'Off with the old and on with the new, eh?' Morton chuckled.

'You could put it like that,' Brad said silkily, replenishing their drinks. 'I think your inestimable secretary needs a holiday. She's worked like a Trojan.'

Morton glanced at Robyn, who looked at him beseechingly. She had not yet had a chance to talk to him privately, and hoped he had not forgotten the reputation she had given herself.

'She plays like a Trojan too,' Morton answered his most illustrious author, and Robyn breathed a sigh of relief.

Not so Brad. He scowled into his glass, then set it down with a bang on the table and dived into the pool.

'What's got into him?' Morton asked, watching Brad thrash through the water.

'The fact that he can't get me,' Robyn said bluntly.

'I see. I'm delighted you're still withstanding him.'

'Only just.'

'Not fallen for him, have you?'

'Teetering,' she confessed.

'Good God!' Morton looked dismayed. 'He's not for you, my dear. He'll break your heart.'

'You don't need to tell me. I'm counting the hours until I can get away.'

'But you'll be able to hold out, won't you?'

'If I find I can't I'll make a dash for it.'

Morton did not smile. 'I'm serious, Robyn.'

'So am I. Now why don't you go up and change? The pool gets the sun until seven, and you'll have time for a swim and a sunbathe.'

'An excellent idea.' He rose and looked around at the colourful mattresses and empty hammocks. 'I was expecting to see the place full of swingers, like the day you arrived.'

'It's only been like that once since,' she admitted. 'I think I rather cramp Brad's style and he goes out for his pleasures!'

Laughing, her employer ambled off to his room. By the time he returned, Robyn was back in the study typing, safe in the knowledge that Brad was out of the way, entertaining his guest.

She did not join them again until dinner, which they ate on the terrace. It was a lovely, leisurely meal, with two excellent wines which Morton Phillips imbibed freely.

'If I could write like you, Brad,' he said, puffing on his

cigar, 'this would be the life for me.'

'You don't do so badly,' Brad drawled. 'You make as much out of my books as I do.'

'I wish I did.'

The banter went on and Robyn listened with half an ear, most of her attention given to Brad, who was becoming more dear to her with each passing day. No wonder each girl-friend agreed that *they* would be the one to make him change his tune.

Fool that she was, she was beginning to think so too.

Stifled by the knowledge, she pushed back her chair. The two men looked at her, neither of them hiding their disappointment when she pleaded a headache and asked to be excused.

In her room she undressed, but made no effort to go to bed, knowing that sleep had never been farther away. From the terrace she heard the soft drone of men's voices, her employer's lighter one and Brad's much deeper. She allowed her mind to drift, reliving the past three weeks, knowing that time would not dim each day, but serve only to enhance it. They would remain, like jewels in a glass case, clear and untarnished, no matter what the future held in store for her.

Eventually she rose and took off her dressing gown. There was no sound from the terrace and she drew the silk curtains to diffuse the morning sunlight when it came in, then padded over to her bed. She had just reached it when there was a tap at the door.

Her heart seemed to jump into her throat. 'Who—who is it?'

'Me—Morton.'

Slipping her dressing gown on again, she inched the door open. Her employer stood there, his face ashen, dark shadows like bruises below his eyes.

'Migraine,' Robyn stated unnecessarily, for he suffered from periodic attacks. 'I knew you shouldn't have mixed your wines tonight. It always brings it on.'

'You sound like my ex-wife,' he groaned. 'You wouldn't have any pills with you? I came away without mine.'

'I only have aspirin, but I've a feeling Mrs Kim has some codeine in the kitchen. Go back to bed and I'll get them.'

He staggered off and Robyn ran silently down the stairs, filmy nylon skirts floating around her. Luckily she found what she was looking for in a small cupboard in the butler's pantry, where Kim, used to dealing with the hang-overs of Bradley Dexter's guests, kept a plentiful supply of headache powders, indigestion tablets and various other pills. Codeine in hand, she went to her employer's room, which was on the other side of the house.

Like her own, it was furnished French style, but Louis Seize this time, with Aubusson carpet and brocade cur-tains to match the coverlet on the fourposter bed. Morton Phillips was lying supine upon it, but roused himself to swallow the pills she handed him with a glass of water.

'Damn stupid of me to get an attack like this,' he muttered. 'Sorry to be such a nuisance, Robyn, but it wasn't the wine that caused it. It was worrying over you. Last thing I want is for you to be hurt by Brad.' He tried to sit up again and groaned.

'Would you like me to massage your shoulders and neck?' Robyn volunteered, remembering she had done so once before when he had been laid low in the office with a similar attack.

'Would you?' he asked gratefully, and rolled over upon his stomach.

With skilful hands Robyn massaged the tensed muscles, kneading them with her fingers until they relaxed and smoothed out. She had never been taught how to do this, but had a natural aptitude which she had discovered in her teens. It had been a toss-up whether she had become a secretary or a physiotherapist, but she had finally opted for the former, knowing that with shorthand and typing she could travel anywhere in the world without having to take further qualifying examinations. Not that she had done much travelling to date, held back as she was by deep affection for her parents, who would miss her regular monthly visits were she to go to America or Australia, the two countries which appealed to her most.

'You have healing hands, my dear,' Morton said in a relaxed voice. 'I feel much better now.'

She drew away from him, only then becoming aware of the perspiration on her forehead and the dampness between her breasts. 'I've left you two more codeine tablets on the bedside table in case you need them,' she said.

There was no reply and she knew he had fallen asleep. Turning off the light, she glanced at the bed again, then stepped back out of the room, straight into a pair of hard, muscular arms. She stifled a shriek and twisted round.

'Sleepwalking?' asked Brad, voice low and sarcastic.

'Mr Phillips had a headache.'

'As real as yours was?'

'Are you calling me a liar?'

'Do I need to?'

Rage overwhelmed her and she stamped her foot, delighted to find it came down hard on his, which was an extra bonus.

His hands fell away from her and he gave a groan of pain. 'You bitch!'

'That's for calling me a liar! We're not all tarnished with the same brush, Bradley Dexter. Mr Phillips did have a headache and I——'

'Spare me the *Mr* Phillips bit,' he said wearily. 'When Morton and I were talking downstairs I asked him how well he knew you, and his leer made it pretty obvious.'

Robyn was silent, for the first time wishing her employer had not entered so wholeheartedly into her deception.

'So what?' she asked pertly, trying to brazen her way out of a situation that was becoming more distressing to her than amusing. 'I never pretended to be an ice-maiden, did I?'

'You pretended you never mixed business with pleasure.'

'I . . . I—er—I stopped seeing Morton when I started working for him. Now we're just good friends.'

'What was tonight's little episode?' The dark head nodded to the door behind her. 'An attack of amnesia?'

'No,' she said furiously. 'Migraine. But you don't believe me.'

'You're damn right I don't! You're no better than—than——'

'Than you are?' she asked sweetly, and sidestepping him, ran down the corridor to the stairhead and then across it to her own room.

Brad and Morton Phillips were having breakfast on the patio when she joined them there the following morning.

'Sleep well, my dear?' the older man asked avuncularly, giving her a theatrical wink which made her long to slap him. How could Brad believe such a monstrous piece of acting?

But that he did was apparent from the tight set of his mouth. Yet why should she care what he thought of her? she asked herself, sipping her coffee with a calmness she did not feel. If he thought badly of her, he would be more likely to leave her alone. The trouble was she didn't want to be left alone. Oh, what a muddle everything was, and how she wished Bradley Dexter had only remained a photograph on the back of a book jacket instead of a flesh-and-blood man who unknowingly held her heart in his uncaring hands.

'There's no need for you to drive me to the airport, old chap,' Morton Phillips' voice broke into her thoughts, and she saw that he was glancing at his watch and moving away from the table.

'You're not going back so soon?' she asked, dismayed.

'Needs must. I couldn't really spare the time to come down here, but I felt I had to, being in Paris and all that.'

He touched Robyn's cheek and she made herself smile at him. Damn Bradley Dexter! Let him believe the worst of her. After all, it couldn't be any worse than the picture she had painted of herself.

'Let *me* drive you to the airport,' she volunteered, twining her arm through his.

'We have work to do,' Brad said behind her. 'I'm sure Morton won't mind if Kim takes him.'

Watching her employer drive away, Kim at the wheel of the Ferrari, Robyn wished she was sitting beside him and leaving the villa for good; except that it wouldn't be for good but for bad.

Fixing a bright smile to her lips, she swung round to the tall, dark man beside her.

'Back to the grindstone, eh?'

'An appropriate simile.' He strode ahead of her up the stairs. 'We certainly manage to strike sparks off one another!' He stopped so abruptly that she bumped into him and he put out a swift hand to steady her. His eyes studied her face, which was devoid of make-up. 'Beats me how you can still look so innocent.'

She made herself give a trill of laughter. 'What do I have to feel guilty about? I never go out with married men, only single ones.'

'How many single ones have there been?'

'This year?'

With an exclamation he turned his back on her and marched up the rest of the stairs. For a brief instant Robyn watched the angry set of his shoulders. Brad was jealous; there could be no other reason for his behaviour last night and today. Come to think of it, it was the only possible explanation for a great deal of his behaviour to her. This advocate of the love-'em-and-leave-'em school, who warned his disciples to run a mile if they felt them-selves beginning to feel tenderly towards a woman, was so riddled with jealousy about her that he was too blind to see what was happening to him. It was a wonderful thought and she hugged it close, refusing to consider whether a leopard could change its spots. The romantic side of her nature, which had kept her single until the right man came along, now made her believe that once Brad discovered how he felt, he would see how shallow all his previous love affairs had been.

'Well, don't just stand there,' he barked from the end of the corridor. 'You're my secretary, remember?'

He did not let her forget it for the rest of the day, once again dictating non-stop, with the minimum break for lunch, during which he went to his room and she heard his deep voice talking on the telephone. The thought that he might be arranging to see another girl depressed her until she remembered that even if he did realise he was in love, he would still fight against it. After all, what shark would willingly have his teeth pulled? She was smiling at the thought when he returned to the study, and though Brad noticed it and gave her a sharp look, he made no comment.

Promptly at six he stood up. 'I've a few friends coming for dinner and I want to have a sleep before they arrive— you look as if you need it too—alone.'

Robyn made herself yawn prettily. 'I am tired, now you mention it, I think I'll have dinner in my room.'

'No, you won't. I'll expect you downstairs at eight-thirty. That's an order.'

Deciding it was wiser not to refuse—besides, if Brad was beginning to care for her she must play the advantage for all it was worth—she spent the intervening hours luxuriating in a bath before making herself look her prettiest.

But it was an inadequate word to describe the ethereal

creature who drifted out to the terrace promptly at half past eight. There were some dozen men and women already there, the men of varying ages, the women all young and decorative, with Holly the centrepiece. But none of them could hold a candle to Robyn. Tall, slender and blonde, in a simple white silk dress with narrow straps holding up the bodice, she made every other female look overdressed and tawdry.

'Well, well, if it isn't Miss Purity herself,' Holly giggled, flashing Brad a look. 'How does she manage to stay that way working with you, darling?'

'Looks are deceptive,' he drawled.

Ignoring them both, Robyn moved across to accept a tomato juice from Kim, who looked at her impassively. But as her fingers curled around the crystal glass, he gave her the faintest of smiles, as if to say that no matter what anyone said about her, he did not believe it. If only Brad had as much sense!

She went to stand against one of the pillars, putting a little distance between herself and the rest of the party, and debating how to behave during the rest of her stay here. Her intention of telling Brad the truth about herself was no longer feasible, for bearing in mind his feelings for her, he might run a mile if he discovered she was an innocent. No, he needed to fall more heavily before she dared risk exposure.

There was a step behind her and Martin came into view. She had not expected him and she warmed to his presence, thinking that with him at least she could let some of her guard down. He still had his arm in a sling and she noticed that the parting of his sandy hair was slightly crooked, as if he could not comb it properly with his left hand.

'How much longer do you have to wear your cast?' she asked.

'Ten days or so. I should be ready to start work in about a month.'

'I bet you'll be pleased?'

'Won't you be? Then you can return to your old job and your old friend.'

She knew immediately that Brad had told him what had happened last night, and angry colour suffused her face. Damn all these men with their double standards! Martin had tried as hard as Brad to seduce her, yet here he was acting annoyed because he believed she was having an affair with someone else.

'The one thing I like about older men,' she said coldly, 'is that they generally have more sense than to sit in judgment upon one.'

'I'm not judging you.' Martin looked startled, as if the idea had not crossed his mind.

'Of course you are—just the way Brad's been doing! And I'd like to inform you—the way I did him—that what I do with my life is no concern of yours.'

'I wanted to make it my concern,' he reminded her. 'I thought you were a sweet girl who——'

'I'm still a sweet girl,' she cut in. 'Why should my character change merely because I—because I'm fond of Mr Phillips?'

'Do you go to bed with every man you're fond of?'

She drew a steadying breath and held on to her temper. 'I was fond of you, but I said no.'

There was a long pause and Robyn, deciding that if the rest of the evening was going to be like this she would go to her room, was on the verge of moving away when Martin spoke.

'Forgive me, Robyn. You're quite right—it's the old double standard, isn't it?'

'That's what I said to Brad,' she agreed.

'Will you forget everything I just said and let me begin again?'

Although she was ready to forgive him, she did not want him to think he could resume their friendship where it had left off. What she felt for Brad made that impossible.

'Of course I'll forgive you,' she murmured. 'But once I leave here, I think it's best if we don't meet.'

'That's hardly very forgiving,' he said ruefully.

'I don't want to hurt you, Martin. I can never be serious about you, and it isn't fair to let you think otherwise.'

'Thanks for the honesty.' He raised his glass to her, drained it, and moved over to get another. He did not return to her and she watched him settle himself next to a pert little brunette.

Relieved, yet faintly depressed, Robyn had the feeling she was going to be left very much to herself for the rest of the evening. Taking a quick count of the people on the terrace, she saw she was the odd girl out, and was convinced Brad had deliberately arranged it this way. Her eyes rested on him. He seemed completely immersed with Holly, who was snuggling up to him. Even at dinner the girl barely allowed herself to be separated from his side; reaching out from time to time to hold his hand and occasionally jumping up from her chair to kiss him. If Brad liked his girl-friends to play the ingénue, then Holly was filling the part beautifully.

At eleven they all trooped out, roaring away in their cars to the casino.

'Care to join us?' Brad asked, sauntering over to her. His face was slightly flushed, though she knew he had not been drinking. Indeed, she was surprised at how abstemious he had been.

'No, thanks,' she shrugged. 'I'd be in the way.'

'I can cope with more than one woman.'

'I can't.'

'I know,' he muttered, turning away. 'You prefer two men!'

Robyn was still puzzling over this when she went to bed, and it was only as she turned off the light that she realised he was referring to Hamish and Alex. She burst out laughing. So Brad still remembered that ridiculous story she had fabricated for him soon after her arrival. How furious he would be if he ever met her mother's adorable little Scotties; silver-haired Alex and his black-haired, sprightly son Hamish.

But her amusement did not last long, for as the hours ticked away, imagination kept her with Brad. He was trying to fight his feelings for her by going out with other women, and she must be careful not to let him know that she guessed the emotions he was experiencing.

Sitting up in bed in the darkness, she wondered what would happen when she left here. Without her presence he would find it much easier to put her out of his mind. It was an unpalatable prospect, and she debated ways and means of remaining here longer. But eventually she discarded them all, knowing it was dangerous to force his hand. If out of sight meant out of mind, then what he felt for her could not be the emotion she wanted. But she still had two more weeks to entwine herself into his subconscious. Two more weeks to strengthen the feelings she aroused in him—not the obvious one of desire, but the deeper ones of affection, mutual interests, shared humour.

Unwilling to stay awake until he returned, Robyn took a sleeping pill—something she rarely did. But at least this way she would not be aware if he stayed out all night.

CHAPTER EIGHT

FOR the next few days Brad altered his system of work, dictating in the morning and allowing her to type for the rest of the day, while he entertained by the pool. The villa seemed to be continually full of people, many of the faces changing, and Holly's being replaced too. Indeed, she never saw Brad with the same girl twice. Most nights he dined at home with a few friends, but Robyn refused to accept his invitation to join them, and he did not insist on it, though each morning he always told her of the fun she had missed.

Coming downstairs early one morning at the end of the week and seeing smashed glass on the living-room floor, which Kim was busy sweeping up, she marvelled that a man of intelligence could consider such behaviour fun.

'It must have been quite an evening,' she commented.

'Mr Dexter not have many like this.' Kim swept up the rest of the mess. 'But he go sleep early and leave his friends.'

Robyn was aflame with jealousy, wondering which one of the girls had distracted him sufficiently to take him away from his own party, but she did not give herself away by asking Kim.

At nine o'clock she was waiting for Brad in the study, but it was nearly ten before he appeared, moving down the spiral staircase as if he were treading on eggshells.

'Alka-Seltzer's excellent for a hangover,' she said brightly.

'I don't have a hangover.' He eased himself slowly into his chair. 'It's fibrositis. I woke up with it.'

'Fibrositis? You're joking!'

'It's no joke.'

She saw the tension on his face, and knew that it wasn't. 'Massage is very good for it.'

'I know. I generally have some twice a week, but my masseuse is on holiday.'

'I can give you some,' Robyn volunteered, and prayed that the colour would not come into her face as he raised his eyes and gave her a long, thoughtful look.

'What kind?'

'Regular,' she said evenly.

'Okay, I'll accept the offer.' Gingerly he stood up. 'It's better if I lie on my bed.'

This was not what she had expected, and she held back, which he was immediately aware of.

'For God's sake,' he said roughly. 'I'm in no mood for lovemaking!'

Instantly she preceded him to his room, waiting while he took off his shirt, undid the belt of his slacks and lay face down on the bed.

Robyn began to massage him. To begin with she was uncomfortably aware of the silky smoothness of his skin, the rippling muscles across his shoulders and the firm thickness of his neck where the dark hair curled. But as the tenseness left his body and he relaxed under the pressure of her hands, she relaxed too, until finally he was only a human being in pain; one whose suffering she could alleviate. She was reminded of the night she had gone to Morton Phillips' room and wondered whether to tell this to Brad. She bent closer, but as her lips parted she saw a long red hair on the far pillow.

She jerked back as though she had been stung.

'What's the matter?' he asked sleepily.

'Nothing.'

Making her mind a blank, she continued the massage until his even breathing told her he was asleep. Only then did she return to the study and allow her emotions free rein. Fool! she berated herself. What did you think Brad would do? He was fighting his feelings in the only way he knew how, and it was stupid of her to imagine he would draw back from the final physical act.

By the time Brad returned to work she had complete control of herself again, and greeted him with her usual composure.

'You have magic hands,' he smiled. 'I feel better than new. Next time I'm in pain I'll give you a yell straight away.'

'Next time don't cavort around in the bedroom with the windows wide open. Draughts are bad for fibrositis.'

'What's *your* icy little blast in aid of?' he questioned, looking so pleased with himself that she longed to slap him.

'Shall we start work, Brad? We've missed most of the morning already.'

With unusual meekness he obeyed her, and even when splashes and screams from the pool announced that his friends had arrived, he did not go down to join them. It was Robyn herself who suggested they stop, saying she had a mass of typing to get back, and that in any case a swim would be good for his shoulder.

'By the way,' he said casually, 'Dick Summers is coming down with Jackie Lawson on Saturday. He's the man who's producing my current book for television, and Jackie's the girl who's playing the feminine lead,' he explained. 'So I wonder if you'd mind doing some overtime this evening and tomorrow? That way there's a good chance I'll finish the book in a week.'

'An excellent idea,' said Robyn, hiding her dejection.

'I thought it was part of your plan to remain here for a month?' he reminded her sardonically.

'So it was. But I'm getting restless.'

'You'll like Dick. Perhaps you'll make up a foursome with us.'

'I'm sure Mr Summers would prefer to choose his own partner.'

Brad smiled. 'He has a penchant for natural blondes.'

A loud squeal from the garden below sent him to lean out of the window. 'Damn stupid girls! Can't think why I invited them here.'

'Old habits die hard,' said Robyn.

'What's that supposed to mean?'

'Merely that if you've grown up enough to find them tedious, you should also be intelligent enough to admit it.'

He frowned, but did not comment on her statement. 'Stop the analysis and to be ready to start work again in an hour. I'll tell my friends to clear off and ask Mrs Kim to serve us a cold supper at nine. Something simple so that we can work and eat.'

Robyn welcomed the break and rested on her bed. She did not return to the study until the appointed time, and found Brad already waiting for her. The garden was silent, all his friends having departed, and she wondered whether she could have a quiet dip later that night before going to bed.

'Ready to start?' Brad asked.

She turned from the desk, where she had placed her notepad, and found him directly behind her. Their bodies touched briefly before she moved quickly away, but she was painfully conscious of the solid feel of him. It was like coming up against a wall of muscle: firm and unbending as the man himself. How foolish all her dreams about him were! He was far too strong to give in to love. Biting back a sigh, she sat down and motioned that she was ready to start work.

They did not stop until nine, when Kim wheeled in a trolley heavy with dishes. There was the most delicious-looking cold asparagus soup, lobster salad, cornets of ham stuffed with artichokes and foie gras, and button mushrooms in cream.

'Some snack,' Robyn said dryly. 'Mrs Kim obviously doesn't like to think of you working on an empty stomach.'

'If she gets any more motherly I'll fire her.'

'You wouldn't!'

'Don't bet on it. I hate motherly women and I don't need anyone to concern themselves over me.'

The lobster, though delicious, tasted like ashes in Robyn's mouth. Had Brad made this remark as a warning to her? Yet he couldn't have done, for she was certain she had not given herself away. Nervous in case he remarked on her lack of appetite, she made herself finish the meal, noticing irritably that Brad had no difficulty in consuming all the food Kim had brought them. Yet she noticed an odd restlessness about him, and wondered if it came from a desire to be with his friends rather than at work.

It was with him the next day too, and occasionally in the midst of dictating to her, he would get up and wander around the room, or else stop work completely for a few moments—the expression on his face showing that his thoughts were far away.

But towards the evening his spirits seemed to revive and he went briskly on with his work until ten, at which time Robyn herself insisted that they stop.

'Are you sure Martin broke his wrist, or did it just give out after working for you for too long?'

'All you needed to do was say you were tired,' Brad replied loftily.

'I've been sighing deeply and shaking my hand for the last hour, but you didn't take the hint.'

'I dislike women who hint. You should have had the courage to come out and say exactly what you meant.'

'I usually do,' Robyn asserted.

'That's true, though I find your attitude somewhat inconsistent. Considering you're supposed to admire the philosophies my books propound, you're singularly unfriendly towards their creator.'

'I dote on Michel Guerard's cookery books,' she replied, 'but I don't think he'd be my type either!'

'Probably not,' Brad grunted. 'You prefer older men.'

She tossed back her blonde hair. 'Not always. Sometimes I——'

'Spare me a history of your love life,' he cut in, striding towards the staircase. 'I think I'll have an early night.' At the top, he paused. 'I'll expect you to join Dick and Jackie for lunch tomorrow, and if you and Dick hit it off, you can consider yourself free to spend your time with him until they go back on Sunday.'

Before Robyn could think of a reply, the door closed behind him.

The next morning she started typing the work Brad had dictated to her during the past two days. He had worked at such a pace that her mind had been too pre-occupied getting the shorthand down to absorb the words themselves. But now, seeing them before her, she found the humour less sharp. It was still amusing, but some of the bite had gone, as if he had found it a strain to find something new to say. Still, how much longer could he go on expounding the same theme? She was curious to know if he was aware of what was happening to his writing. Could this be the reason for his moodiness of the past few days? She must talk to Morton Phillips about it when she returned home, for he had frequently stressed the hope that his best-selling author would put his talents into a novel.

At mid-morning the sound of laughter from the terrace told her that the two guests had arrived. She was curious to meet them, and wondered idly whether the television star had been one of Brad's girl-friends. If she wasn't, she soon would be, if his present behaviour was anything to go by.

Resolutely she tried to ignore the splashing in the pool and the faint sound of music, and it was only when Kim came in and told her she was expected downstairs that she glanced at her watch and saw it was nearly one o'clock.

It was no surprise to Robyn when she finally walked on to the terrace to find Brad sitting alongside a svelte, raven-haired beauty who she knew immediately was Jackie Lawson. Perched a few feet away was a pleasant-looking man in his late thirties, with grizzled grey hair and a slightly darker beard. Though not as tall as Brad, he was well built and took her hand in a firm grip as Brad laconically made the introductions.

'I can see why Brad broke his rule about not having a female secretary,' Dick Summers smiled. 'You're a great improvement on Martin!'

'A temporary one only,' she smiled, helping herself to a fruit juice, and then standing irresolute, not sure where to sit. The problem was resolved by Brad jumping up and saying there was just time for a swim before lunch.

'Count me out,' Jackie said firmly.

'What about you?' Brad challenged Robyn.

'I'd love it.' Setting down her glass, she followed him down to the pool.

'Such energy,' said Dick behind her. 'I'll come and watch you two.'

Reaching one of the mattresses, Robyn dropped her jacket on it, ignoring the appreciative way Dick regarded her.

'Race you to the end,' Brad said curtly. 'I'll give you a two-yard start.'

'Right,' she said, and plunged in, knowing that even with this advantage, she still would not win, and she was proved correct when, half way down the length of the pool, Brad overtook and passed her.

'I'm much too good for you,' he grinned when she finally reached the side and hauled herself up on the ledge beside him.

'Only in the pool!'

'Naturally!'

Robyn caught a length of her hair and wrung it out.

Even darkened by water it was still fair, and when she shook her head, the long strands curved upon her shoulders.

'You look like a mermaid,' he said abruptly.

'I don't have quite such a fishy background!'

He laughed. 'Tell me about it.'

'I've already told you. Elderly parents who doted on me and somehow managed not to spoil me, and were never too possessive. Quite an unexciting past really, but a pleasant one.'

'And your future?'

'I've told you about that too. The female equivalent of yours, Brad—fun without commitment.'

'You won't always be young,' he reminded her.

'Nor will you.'

'It's different for a man. And don't pretend it isn't. I'm not talking about double standards either, merely the obvious fact that even middle-aged men can find young women.'

'I'll worry about that when the time comes,' Robyn said airily. 'But as you know, I intend starting a family in five years' time, so I'll be quite happy to devote myself to my children.'

'And give up men?'

'That won't be a hardship,' she said firmly. 'You know what a low opinion I have of them.'

For answer he pushed her into the pool, and when she rose she floated effortlessly away from him.

At lunch, Brad and his two guests talked about the forthcoming television series. Several problems had arisen with the scripts, which was the reason Dick Summers had come down, though it was soon clear that Jackie's presence had not been required, and she had merely come to renew her friendship with Brad, whom she had met three years ago in New York.

'Those were the days,' she reminisced, raising her wine

glass to him. 'You rented that fantastic house on Fire Island and filled it with girls.' She glanced the length of the table, then let her eyes roam the long terrace, with its empty hammocks and chairs. 'What happened to the old Brad?'

'Perhaps he's bored with the old ways?' Dick chuckled.

'Just bored with the same faces,' Brad corrected, raising his own glass to toast Jackie. 'Which is why I'm delighted to renew acquaintance with you.'

The girl laughed. 'At least if I'm nice to you, you'll know it isn't because I need a part in your new series!'

He grinned. 'You mean you'll love me for myself?'

'I always did, but you refused to believe me.'

Robyn had the feeling that Jackie was not putting on an act. She had warmed to the girl as soon as she had met her, and had found no reason to change her mind since.

'Before you two start becoming too palsy-walsy,' Dick intervened, 'I'm taking Brad off somewhere quiet to discuss the alterations to the scripts.'

'Will you need me?' Robyn asked.

'No,' Brad said swiftly. 'I'll use the tape recorder.'

As soon as lunch was over, the two men disappeared to the study, and Robyn, unable to go back and type, sat under the shade of a parasol with Jackie, and occasionally swam in the pool. Unlike Brad's other girl-friends, Jackie was intelligent and articulate, which was probably one reason why Brad had not seen her for the last three years.

'I daresay you'll be sorry to go back to London?' Jackie murmured, rubbing oil on her slim thighs.

'Not really. Being here is fine for a holiday, but I prefer my other job.'

'To working for Brad?' There was astonishment in the dark brown eyes. 'I'd give my eye teeth if I could find a good reason for staying close to him.'

'Don't let him know it,' Robyn warned.

'Don't worry. I had lover-boy taped three years ago

and he still hasn't changed—unfortunately.' There was a pause, and when Jackie spoke again her voice had brightened. 'Still, when he knew Dick was coming down he asked him to bring me, so perhaps absence has made the heart grow fonder.'

Robyn swallowed her jealousy, and lay back on her mattress, pretending she wanted to sleep. She actually managed to do so, and did not awaken until she felt the pressure of a foot on her stomach. Opening her eyes, she saw Dick beaming down at her.

'All problems have been resolved,' he said happily. 'So until my plane takes off tomorrow night, I'm at your disposal.'

'That goes for me too,' said Brad, coming up behind the producer but directing his comment at Jackie, who reached out a lazy arm for him.

He stretched himself out beside her, and Robyn could not help noticing that the two bodies were both tanned the same magnificent bronze, and that Jackie's hair was as blue-black as Brad's own. The two could have passed for brother and sister, though Jackie clearly did not feel sisterly towards him. But what did Brad feel? His hand was idly caressing the supple leg lying close to his, and Robyn turned away, ostensibly to sun her back, but in reality because she could not bear the sight of Brad so intimately close to another woman.

She knew it was going to be even worse this evening when she was expected to dine with them and then go out, but she could see no way of avoiding it without having an argument with Brad. Besides, what excuse could she give?

It was only when she came downstairs and saw the dining table unlaid that she realised they were eating out, and the second shock came when she walked on to the terrace and saw that only Dick Summers was there.

'You're stuck with me, I'm afraid.' He rose to greet her.

'I hope you don't feel I'm getting the best of the bargain?'

'To dine alone with a well-known television producer?' she teased, determined not to let him know how annoyed she was with Brad for going off alone with Jackie and leaving them. Yet she had no right to be annoyed, and no girl in her right mind would. After all, what could be nicer than dining tête-à-tête with an attractive man who made it clear how happy he was to be with you?

'I've booked us a table at l'Oasis,' he said. 'In my opinion it's the best three-star restaurant along the coast.' He eyed her bare shoulders, rising honey-gold from the low cut neckline of a leaf-green dress. 'You look as delectable as a mint julep,' he added, leaning towards her.

'An iced mint julep,' she replied, and he laughed and drew back.

'Let's have a drink in the restaurant,' he suggested, and led her out to the Fiat. 'Not as grand as the Ferrari,' he apologised, 'but Brad's more possessive of that than he is of his girl-friends.'

Dick stopped, embarrassed, and Robyn shook her head at him. 'I only have a working relationship with Brad, so you haven't embarrassed me.'

'I refuse to believe he hasn't made a pass at you.'

'He has—but *I* passed it up! And please don't tell me that it makes me unique.'

Chuckling, he helped her into the car and they set off in the direction of Cannes. Dick was an entertaining companion. He had worked in television since leaving university, beginning as a lowly second assistant and gradually learning his craft, until now he was acknowledged to be one of the top producers in the country.

'Have you ever thought of being an actress?' he asked as they ate a superlative meal, sitting in the enclosed courtyard of the elegant restaurant in La Napoule, where fountains tinkled and flowers cascaded over low walls and flower beds.

'I don't have the talent for it,' she confessed, 'nor the

inclination. Not every girl sees it as such a glamorous occupation.'

'It's not glamorous at all,' he agreed. 'But if you're successful it can be very well paid. Take Jackie for example. She has a small talent but a great personality, and she plays it up for all she's worth. But once her looks go, she might not find it easy to get work.'

'She may not need work by then.'

'Not if Brad comes up to scratch,' Dick said knowingly. 'Jackie's been crazy about him for years. That's why I'm surprised he invited her down this weekend. He usually steers clear of a woman if he knows she's keen on him. Nor have I ever known him restart an old love affair.'

Dick's remarks were guaranteed to add to Robyn's disquiet. What if all the barbs she had directed at Brad over the past few weeks had made him see the emptiness of his life and decided him to turn to Jackie? She was certainly the nicest of his girl-friends. Robyn was so depressed by the idea that it was an effort for her to hide it. But the fear of giving herself away made her put on the best act of her life—even though she had told Dick she was no actress—and she laughed and joked with him as if he were the one person in the world with whom she wanted to be: as if she were not wondering where Brad had taken Jackie to dine; as if she did not care where he would be taking her to sleep.

The red Ferrari was already in the garage when Dick parked the Fiat, but neither Brad nor Jackie were to be seen downstairs, and when Dick suggested Robyn have a nightcap with him, she refused.

'I'd like to see you again in London,' he said, pausing on the stairs with her before going in the opposite direction to his room. 'May I call you?'

She smiled and nodded, then let him kiss her goodnight. His lips were gentle, but she could not respond to them, nor did she pretend.

Alone in her bedroom at last, she gave way to the despondency she had been fighting all evening, and kicking off her shoes she flung herself into a chair. How crazy she had been to imagine she could succeed with Brad, when so many other girls had failed. Falling in love with him was the worst thing that could have happened to her. The sooner she was home, in her old job among her own friends, the sooner her weeks here would seem like time spent in another world. If only she could go back to London tomorrow with Jackie and Dick! Still, another week should have the story finished, and then she would be free.

Wearily she undressed and went to bed.

Robyn had nearly finished her breakfast when Jackie came out to join her. Crisp and cool-looking in a cream silk suit, her black hair was held away from her face by a gold and tortoiseshell clip. It threw the bone structure of her face into relief, and Robyn realised she was not as young as she had first thought: early thirties rather than late twenties.

'I hear you and Dick enjoyed yourselves last night,' said Jackie, ignoring the flaky croissants and pouring herself a cup of coffee.

'We had a wonderful meal.' Robyn made herself enthuse. 'What about you?'

'Brad took me to La Réserve.'

Robyn lowered her eyes. So much for her romantic notion that Brad might not want to take anyone there but herself! 'It's a lovely restaurant,' she murmured.

'Which is more than I can say for Brad. He was in a foul mood. I've never known him act that way. And he got worse as the evening went on.'

'Is that why you came back early?'

'Yes. I thought Brad might improve when I got him alone, and——'

'Don't be long, Jackie,' Dick called from the doorway. 'Brad's taking us to the airport.'

'I'm packed and ready.' Jackie went towards him and Dick smiled over her shoulder to Robyn.

'See you in London,' he promised, and might have said more had Brad not appeared behind him.

To Robyn's sharp eyes he looked like the morning after the night before. His face lacked its normal healthy colour, which gave his tan a greenish tinge, and there were noticeable lines around his eyes. But the dissipation made him look even more attractive, and Robyn quickly turned her eyes away from him and smiled at Dick.

'I should be back in town in just over a week. I'll look forward to hearing from you.'

'I'm not sure what time I'll be home,' Brad said curtly to her as Dick and Jackie went out to the car.

'It doesn't matter. I've got plenty of shorthand to get back.'

'Then I may go away for the night.'

'Why not?' she said sweetly, and walked past him.

Robyn typed for most of the day, stopping for a short spell at lunch and tea time to swim and relax by the pool. The villa seemed large and empty without Brad, but she resolutely refused to wonder what he was doing, knowing that wherever he was, he would not be alone.

The thought came back to worry at her as she ate a solitary meal in the dining room. A breeze had sprung up in the late afternoon, growing in intensity and making it necessary for Kim to close all the glass doors and wind in the awnings.

'We have storm coming,' he announced. 'Like tropics.'

Hardly had he spoken when rain began to fall, accompanied by a jagged flash of lightning. Remembering she had left her bedroom window wide open, Robyn rushed upstairs to close it; then deciding to have an early night, she undressed, put on her dressing gown and curled up on a seat beside the window to watch the storm.

Because the house was situated some few hundred yards from the cliff, she could not see the shore that edged Cap d'Antibes, but she had an excellent view of the wider curve of the bay and of the foaming Mediterranean beyond it. It looked as wild as the Atlantic, and jagged streaks of lightning frequently illuminated the dark waters, turning the landscape into day for a few brief seconds. As each bright flash died away, thunder roared, telling her that she was almost in the heart of the storm. Just like my own heart, she admitted wearily.

She was not sure how long she had been sitting by the window, when the door to her bedroom burst open and Brad stood on the threshold. One look at his face told her he had been drinking; not enough to lessen his control, but enough to make her realise she had to tread carefully if she did not want to antagonise him.

'All alone?' he sneered. 'Don't tell me you can't find yourself a man.'

'I don't want one.' She kept her voice mild. 'I've been watching the storm. It's beautiful.'

'So are you.' He came farther into the room, slamming the door behind him. 'Look at me when I'm talking to you!' he said roughly. '*I'm* the storm you should be watching. But you wouldn't know about that, would you?'

'Know about what?'

Something in his manner increased her nervousness. He came closer to her, his steps making no sound across the floor. His wide shoulders blacked out the soft light of the bedside lamp, and she resisted the urge to cower in her chair. There was something wild about Brad tonight; something untamable.

'About the reason for my mood,' he answered her question. 'Why I'm raging like a storm inside; why I haven't known any peace for days, for weeks, if you must know the truth. Don't you know what you've done to me?'

'I'm sure you're going to tell me.' Robyn forced herself to look directly at him. His eyes were glittering and his mouth was tightly set. She was not sure what he was trying to tell her and refused to let herself hope.

'At first I thought it was because you were playing hard to get,' he went on. 'I thought it was because I didn't like being rejected by a girl who was quite happy to give her favours indiscriminately to everyone else.'

'I've been exceptionally discriminating since I've been here,' she said with perfect truthfulness, wishing she dared confess she was the same in London.

'What about the chap in Monte Carlo?' he retorted. 'And the night you spent with Morton. Or don't they count?'

'I wasn't alone with Pierre.' She decided to be truthful about this. 'If you must know, he's married and his wife——'

'Spare me the sordid details!' Brad cut in furiously. 'All I'm interested in is your own future.'

Hope rose in her, high as a flame in the wind. But she was still determined not to push him into anything. Brad must make all the running, and only when he had admitted he loved her would she tell him the truth about herself.

'It's your future I'm concerned with,' he repeated. 'Your future with *me*.'

'With you?'

'Don't tell me you're surprised! You've been baiting me since you got here and you've finally hooked me. Oh, I fought against you—you can take my word on that.' There was frustration in his voice. 'But it didn't work. The more I got to know you the more difficult it was to get you out of my mind.'

'Why are you so angry about it?' she asked.

'Because I don't want to feel this way about any

woman. Until now I never gave a damn which girl I was with. All I wanted was someone who could amuse me and was pretty to look at. Not that I ever found one who could amuse me for long,' he admitted. 'But what the heck! It was off with the old and on with the new.' He glowered at her. 'At least that's the way it was until you erupted into my life. You, with your sharp tongue and pretended hero-worship.'

'Pretended?' she echoed.

'Yes,' he said flatly. 'Quoting my books back at me all the time, making out you thought I was the greatest thing since sliced bread, but really despising me—the way you despise all men.'

'Not all of them,' she amended. 'But most of them. The way you despise most women. I don't see why you should be angry with me because I'm the female equivalent of you.'

'I don't know either,' he confessed. 'But I do. I hate the thought of you playing around, and it's got to stop. From now on *I'm* going to be the only man in your life.'

The flame in her rose higher, but still she tried to hide it from him, waiting for him to use the word love; knowing it was inherent in everything he was saying, but that it was important for him to utter the word.

'I knew you were starting to mean something special to me when none of the other girls could make me forget you,' he went. 'Holly just made me furious, and it was no good even with Marcia. I kept seeing your face all the time and hearing your voice. It made me useless with them,' he said bitterly, 'absolutely useless. That's why I asked Jackie down. She's more than just a pretty face. She's a bright girl, the way you are, and I was sure that having her here would do the trick.'

'Didn't it?' Robyn asked softly, slowly daring to believe that what she had been hoping for was finally coming true.

'No, she didn't,' Brad flared. 'All she did was to remind me even more forcibly of you. I couldn't even bring myself to kiss her.' There was disgust in his voice. 'That would make a great story, wouldn't it? The impotent Casanova! But it's true, dammit! Right now I'm no good to any woman except you. Everyone else turns me off. It's never happened to me before and I hope it will never happen to me again once I've got you out of my system.'

'Out of your system?' Robyn repeated, not sure what he meant.

'Yes,' he said. 'That's why I want you to give up your job with Morton and stay with me. I don't think it need be for long. Three months, perhaps six. But I want you to stay until I've had my fill of you.'

'And then?'

'Then you'll be free to go. I know you keep saying I'm not your type, but I'm sure you don't mean it. If you did, you wouldn't respond to me the way you do when I kiss you.' He bent over her chair, his breath fanning her forehead. 'I'm crazy about you, Robyn,' he said huskily. 'You amuse me, intrigue me, infuriate me, provoke me until I don't know whether I'm on my heels or my head. But I'm sure that if I could concentrate on you for the next few months . . . absorb you into my system until you were a part of me, that I'd then be able to get you out of it. It's the cold turkey treatment in reverse.'

Robyn had no need to ask what he meant. Many hospitals treated drug addicts this way: taking the patient completely off the drug to which they were addicted. But Brad wanted to do the opposite. He wanted to have his fill of her; to possess her so completely that he would quickly tire of her.

So much for her hope that he had fallen in love with her! All that had happened was that her refusal to give in to him had turned his conquering instinct into an obsession; had made him so determined to possess her that he was blind to the blandishments of any other woman. Yet how hard he had tried not to be. He had used Holly, Marcia and Jackie to break the spell, and only when they had all failed had he come to her in desperation. 'Stay with me, Robyn,' he said softly. 'If my books mean anything to you, stay with me until I can send you away and carry on with my life.'

Before she had a chance to reply he pulled her up into his arms and claimed her lips with a ferocity that showed he had reached the end of his tether. She was powerless to fight him, and he continued his assault on her senses, crushing her close and moving his hands over her as if he were a blind man intent on knowing every curve and indentation of her body. Uncaring of the buttons that kept her housecoat together, he ripped it apart, leaving her standing before him in brief lacy underwear. She was no more bare than in a bikini, yet because she was in the bedroom and because he was watching her with such naked desire, she felt as if she were totally naked. Worse still, as if she were being violated.

All hope was gone and she saw how futile had been her chance of making him accept an emotion like love. How could he believe in something he had denounced nearly all of his life? She had not played him for a fool, but herself. It was a bitter acknowledgement, but she faced it; faced too the fact that he must never know how much he had hurt her. But oh, how hard it was to pretend.

'I want you,' he muttered thickly. 'Robyn . . . darling . . . don't make me stop now.' He gathered her close again, his tongue tracing a line of fire across her mouth, her closed eyes, the wild pulse beating in her throat. 'With you I can be a man again,' he went on triumphantly. 'You've driven me insane, Robyn, and now you must give me back my sanity. Hold me, darling . . . love me . . .' He put her hands on his body and she felt his heart racing as wildly as her own. He was trembling, too, his desire for her so evident that words were unnecessary.

As he drew her down upon the bed he started to undo his trouser belt, and the gesture acted on her like a knife across her skin. She sat up sharply and slithered away from him.

'No, Brad. Not tonight. Not while I'm still working for you.'

His hands stilled their movement and he looked at her in puzzlement. 'Don't refuse me, Robyn. God, I want you so much, I——'

'Not while I'm working for you,' she interrupted, and reaching for her housecoat, put it on.

'Why the hell not?' he burst out.

'Because I don't mix business with pleasure.'

'What about Morton?'

She went scarlet. 'I . . . that was a little slip. But it won't happen again.' She saw Brad coming towards her and sidestepped him. 'No, Brad, I mean it. If you don't leave me alone I'll go back to England tomorrow.'

Her very quietness told him she was not pretending.

'But when the book's finished?' he asked slowly. 'Will you live with me then?'

'I thought you said a man should never allow a girl to live with him?'

'You'll be the exception—and for God's sake stop quoting my books at me!' He reached out for her hand, though he did not come any nearer to her. 'At least I'll have an incentive to get this manuscript finished as fast as I can!' He drew her fingers to his mouth and gently nibbled them. 'How can you stand there looking so calm?' he whispered.

'Because I *am* calm,' she said, praying he would not guess she was the exact opposite.

'Aren't you looking forward to being with me?' His tongue caressed her fingertips.

'Not particularly.'

The movement of his hand stilled. 'Don't tease me, Robyn. Say something nice.'

'Even though I don't feel it?'

He looked at her, his eyes puzzled. 'You must feel something for me. Damn it, you always respond to me.'

'You kiss with great expertise.'

'Is it no more than that?'

'And you're very famous, of course.'

'What's that got to do with it?'

'A great deal. Being with a celebrity turns me on. I've never had a best-selling author before.'

'That's a disgusting thing to say!'

'That you're an author?'

'That my being a celebrity is the only thing that turns you on.'

'You once said the same thing when you were going out with one of the Miss Worlds.'

To her astonishment a wave of red flooded his cheeks.

'The fact that *I* say it doesn't mean you should,' he said sharply. 'You're talking like a common groupie! Don't you have any respect for yourself?'

'What does my respecting myself have to do with sex?' She was quoting him with a vengeance now, but he did not seem to notice it.

'I don't want you to talk this way, Robyn. Nor do I intend staying here any longer. The next time I come to your room it will be to stay the night.'

'I don't have any mirrors on the ceiling.'

He gave her a long, intent look. 'Looking at you is more than enough for me. I won't need any reflections.'

But Robyn had a great deal to reflect on after Brad had left her, and the saddest one was that though he wanted her enough to ask her to become his live-in girl-friend, which was something he had never done with any woman, he still only saw it as an affair. Many girls would jump at such a chance in the hope that they might be able to extend it, but Robyn dared not. She saw love in terms of total commitment, and could have no future with a man who thought only in the short term.

She slipped on her nightdress and clambered into bed. The touch of Brad's hands still lingered on her body, reminding her of the pleasures they could have shared, the heights they could have reached. But on Brad's part the peaks were of desire, not love, and to have shared them with him would have made her no better than he was. But she must not tell him. She must keep him hoping for another week. Only when the manuscript was finished could she leave and be her own mistress.

That was one thing of which she *was* sure. She would never be Brad's.

CHAPTER NINE

BELIEVING that he could not have Robyn while she was working for him gave Brad exactly the impetus he needed. Instructing Kim that he was not available to take calls from anyone other than his publishers, and that he was home to none of his friends, he wrote with determined ferocity. Robyn, as anxious as Brad to have the book finished—though for a different reason—happily worked till late each night to type back each day's dictation.

On the Thursday, lifting her head from her notebook while he was still speaking, she saw him watching her with a strange expression: a pensive, somewhat puzzled one, as if there was something about her he did not understand.

'You're an odd mixture,' he murmured. 'When you don't know I'm watching you, you have quite a different expression on your face. And you walk differently too. It's hard to imagine you with a past.'

'Do women with a past walk in a different way?'

'You know what I mean.'

'I'm not sure I do.' She hesitated. 'Which image of me do you prefer?'

He did not answer.

'You only have one image for *me*, Brad.'

'A totally black one, I suppose?'

'You've worked hard to get it.'

'For the next six months I'll stop working at it. Once I've sent off the manuscript we'll close the villa and travel.'

'Why?' she asked.

'Because it will be difficult to keep all my friends at bay, and I don't want to share you with anyone.'

'You weren't serious about our being faithful to each other?' she asked with simulated horror, then before he could reply, she gave a trill of laughter. 'Really, Brad! You'd better watch out or you might find you've fallen in love with me.'

'Don't talk rubbish,' he said irritably. 'Anyway, there are different meanings to love.'

'Yours sounds as if it might be possessive.' She hesitated, then said daringly: 'I hope you aren't thinking in terms of marriage?'

This time he was the one to laugh. 'My God, there's no fear of that. I may be crazy with wanting you, but I'm not totally out of my mind!'

Robyn needed no further confirmation to show her what her next step should be, and on Friday night, with the manuscript finally completed, she went to her room and packed her cases. There was no late flight to London, but she had booked one to Paris and was changing there, knowing that to stay in the villa with Brad would be a temptation she could not fight.

She debated whether to leave without telling him, then decided that if she did, he might come after her, seeing her flight as one more sign of provocativeness. Because of this, she went in search of him, overcome with nervousness when she found him in the living room uncorking a bottle of champagne.

'There you are, darling!' he greeted her. 'At least we've got something to celebrate.'

'The end of the book?' she smiled, knowing she would always remember him like this, casually yet expensively clad in well-fitting slacks and Italian silk sweater.

'The end of a book but the beginning of *our* new chapter,' he replied, coming over to her with a brimming glass, then raised his own. 'To us.'

'I'm afraid not.'

The glass was half way to his lips before he heard her,

and he lowered it. Her expression told him she was not joking, and the smile left his face.

'Why not? The book's finished, so you've no reason for refusing to live with me.'

'Yes, I have. Two reasons, as a matter of fact.' Robyn was glad she had rehearsed her story carefully, otherwise her nerve might have failed her.

'Not Morton and Pierre,' said Brad. 'I promise I won't refer to them again.'

'It's got nothing to do with them. It's Hamish and Alex.'

'Hamish and . . . You're having me on!'

'I wish I were,' she said sadly. 'But I'm afraid it's true. I've known them for years—since I was a child, in fact—and I can't imagine my life without them.' She made herself look him full in the face. 'You wouldn't be happy to share me with them, I suppose?'

'No, I wouldn't!' he exploded. 'What sort of a man do you take me for?'

'Well, you're not the man you pretend to be,' she sighed heavily. 'In the last chapter of your book you warn men of the danger of becoming possessive of their girl-friends, yet now, when I suggest you share me, you get all uptight about it.' She set down her glass on the table. 'That's why it won't work for us, Brad. No matter what advice you give to others, you're completely different in your attitude to me. You're not the liberated man I thought you were, and you'd expect me to conform to ideas I consider old-fashioned.'

'Only for six months—I'm not asking for a longer commitment than that. Besides, once you're mine, you won't want anyone else. I know *I* won't.'

'That's why I'm leaving.' She held out her hand. 'It was very interesting meeting you, Brad, but I don't want to stay.'

'You can't go.'

'I can, and I am. Goodbye, Brad.'

Slowly Robyn turned and walked out, wondering if he would say the three words that would make her turn and run into his arms. But he remained silent and unmoving.

Kim had already put her cases in the Fiat and was sitting at the wheel. She climbed in beside him and closed the door. There was still no sign from Brad, and she knew there never would be.

'We'd better go, Kim,' she said evenly. 'I don't want to miss my plane.'

A month later Robyn thought of her stay at the villa as a dream from which she had still not quite awakened. She had telephoned Morton before leaving France and he had met her at the airport, taken the manuscript from her and firmly told her to take a week's holiday with her parents.

'Why with my parents?' she questioned as they bowled along the motorway towards London.

'Because staying with them will help you to get your priorities straightened again.'

'I never lost my priorities—nor my morals.'

'Just your heart? And don't deny it, Robyn. I know you too well for that.'

'I'll recover,' she said tightly. 'Just don't show me any sympathy. Nor do I want a holiday.'

'Brad might come after you,' he ventured.

'Only with the same offer.' Briefly she told him what it had been, and he was too worldly to express surprise.

'You were sensible to turn him down,' he said. 'A lot of other girls in your position might have agreed to do what he wanted and hoped he might make it permanent. But he never would.'

Although Morton Phillips was only echoing Robyn's own belief, she still could not quench the faint hope that they might both be proved wrong, and each time the telephone rang at her flat, or someone called at the office, she would momentarily think it was Brad.

It was only when she opened her breakfast paper one morning two months after her return from France, and read in the gossip column that he had closed his villa and moved to Los Angeles, that she faced the fact that he would never contact her. Well, it was good to finally know it. From now on she had no excuse for false hope and could set about rebuilding her life.

Morton indicated that he was more than happy to help her, and though she relented and went out with him a few times, she knew he could never mean anything to her. Besides, he reminded her of Brad, and because of it she knew she would have to leave him. Yet she was loath to give up a job she enjoyed, especially since he had arranged for another girl to take over his secretarial work; and had given herself manuscripts to read and edit, as well as placing several new authors in her care.

Robyn enjoyed playing wet nurse; being called upon to advise on first drafts of stories which she eventually came to regard with a proprietorial air; correcting the galley proofs as though she had written the books herself.

Within three months she received a substantial increase in salary, and was given the task of finding authors as well as maintaining her present ones. It was not an easy task, for though hundreds of manuscripts were submitted to them each year, less than half a dozen new writers were chosen.

Brad's book and television series were scheduled for the first week in January, and Robyn knew he would be coming to London to promote it. Several chat show producers had already rung to see if he would appear for them, and a literary lunch was being given in his honour.

'How do you feel about meeting him?' Morton asked, coming into the small office she had been given.

'I'd rather not,' she replied, 'but I'm going to.'

'Well, you can count on me for immoral support!'

She laughed. 'I might take you up on it.'

'I wish you meant that,' Morton sighed. 'Incidentally, I'm giving Brad a press party at the Savoy. You'll be there, of course?'

'Of course.'

'Still going to maintain your false image with him?' Morton asked, folding his arms across his chest and looking, in his black pin-striped suit, like a disapproving headmaster.

'I have more reason now than ever,' Robyn replied, swivelling in her chair. It was as new as the chrome and glass desk in front of her, and made her feel much more like the publishing editor she had now become. 'If Brad discovered that my behaviour had been an act, he'd immediately guess I'd fallen for him.'

'You're still down for the count, aren't you?'

She sighed. 'But slowly picking myself up. Seeing him will do me good, particularly if he arrives with one of his usual dolly-birds.'

Four weeks later she had her answer, for Bradley Dexter's arrival in London with a luscious young centrefold from the current *Playboy* made the front page of every tabloid. Looking at his smiling face and the tall, lithe body towering over the busty blonde, she almost hated him. What did he know of insomniac hours, of days of depression, of throwing oneself into work in order to forget a voice, a mannerism, a special glint in a special pair of eyes? Once again the love she felt for him washed over her with renewed force, making a mockery of her earlier assertion that she was beginning to forget him.

If only she had not promised Morton to go to Brad's party at the Savoy! But short of pleading sickness there was no way she could get out of it and, determined to go down fighting, she bought herself a new dress for the occasion.

She had her hair restyled too, going to a hairdresser

who was currently the pet of *Vogue* and *Harpers*. Luckily he seemed happy not to cut her hair and went into rhapsodies over its silvery fairness.

'But you should make it your main feature,' he ordered her. 'I want everyone to focus on it the moment you enter a room.'

'Then you'd best cover up the rest of 'er,' said his assistant, a pert little Cockney girl.

Ignoring the comment, he set to work, snipping and shaping before lightly perming, and leaving Robyn with a mass of eye-catching silver-gilt curls that gave her the air of an adorable cherub. It looked incongrous with her tall, slender figure, and she wondered if she had the courage to wear it this way or would brush it out flat the minute she got home. But within a few hours she was used to it; in fact she enjoyed seeing men stare at her with even stronger interest than they usually did. Let Brad look at her with lust too—that was if he remembered her at all. Let every man regard her that way. Perhaps the day would come when she would meet such a look and be able to return it, thereby forgetting the might-have-beens and finding happiness with someone else.

For the party Robyn wore red; a vivid zinging red, that gave her skin the iridescent sheen of a pearl. The neckline was high, outlining the full curves of her breasts, which owed nothing to a bra, as the low-cut back testified, and the sweeping lines of the skirt made her seem even taller than she was.

'You look beautiful,' said Morton, greeting her with a kiss as she entered the private suite he had booked at the Savoy.

It was already filling with people, though Brad had not yet arrived. But Dick Summers was there, as was Jackie and several other members of the television cast of the series.

'Wow with a capital W!' commented Dick, coming up

to greet her. 'Who's the lucky man who's taking you home tonight?'

'I am,' said Morton, putting a hand lightly but firmly around Robyn's waist.

'How can I fight my host?' Dick asked ruefully.

'You can't. Which puts me in an impregnable position!'

Everyone laughed and Robyn gave Morton a brilliant smile, deeply moved that he should be willing to help her through the next few, painful hours.

An excited murmur from the crowd around them told them that the guest of honour had arrived, and almost at once Bradley Dexter came into view. His publicity photographs don't do him justice, Robyn thought as her heart gave a painful jolt, for they did not show the sheen of his skin nor the raven gleam of his hair. Neither could a camera lens adequately catch the glint in the hazel eyes and the mocking curve of the wide, mobile mouth. He was formally dressed tonight in a dark blue suit that made him look taller and leaner than she remembered him.

He came towards them, smiling coolly at Robyn before turning to greet Morton, then drawing forward the nubile blonde he had brought with him. She was everything one expected a Bradley Dexter girl to be: better stacked physically than mentally, and looking at him with undisguised adoration.

Robyn's fear that he might seek her out later and talk to her alone died as he circulated from one group of journalists to another, always with his companion in tow, though he smilingly put her to one side as he posed for some pictures with Jackie. The evening wore on. Drink flowed more freely than food, and by nine o'clock Robyn was becoming lightheaded.

'Bear up for another half hour,' Morton urged her. 'Then we'll go out to dinner.'

'Not with Brad,' Robyn said tightly. 'I couldn't bear it.'

'Yes, you can. You've done marvellously so far. Have some more champagne, it will make you feel better.'

'It might also make me fall flat on my face!'

'Your *smiling* face,' he ordered, and lightly touched his finger to her lips.

She made a brave effort to smile at him, glad no one else could guess how close to tears she was.

'What's the plan for tonight, Morton?' Brad came up behind them. 'Or am I interrupting a tête-à-tête?'

'Not at all, old chap. I was just telling Robyn we should soon be going. You'll join us, of course? I've booked a table at Les A. Dick and Jackie are coming along.'

'Sounds great,' Brad said easily. 'I'll meet you there.'

But Brad and his girl-friend were the last to arrive at the smart restaurant in Park Lane, and everyone was on their second round of drinks.

'We won't ask what took you so long,' Dick joked, and the blonde giggled and clung to Brad's arm.

Robyn stared down at her glass, musing on what damage it would do if she flung the contents on the sleek hair of the girl in front of her. Brad would probably laugh. After all, he liked having women fight over him.

At dinner, Morton tried to seat everyone so that Brad was as far away from Robyn as possible, and though he succeeded, she found it worse to have him sitting opposite her. Each time she looked up she saw him acting the fool with his even more foolish companion. How could a man of intelligence waste his time with such a dimwit?

'Care to dance?' Morton asked her when they had all given their orders, and she gratefully let him lead her on to the floor; anything to give her a few moments' respite from watching Brad.

Morton was an excellent dancer who thoroughly enjoyed performing intricate steps. It forced Robyn to concentrate on following him, and gave her little time to think of anything else, for which she was thankful. What a pity she couldn't fall in love with someone like Morton; a man who would cherish her and make her feel loved and wanted.

'Do you know this is the first time I've danced with you?' he whispered against her hair. 'I hope you won't let it be the last?'

The warmth in his voice warned her it would be safer if it was. She had nothing to give Morton and she did not wish to use him. But now was not the time to tell him, and she smiled and made no answer, glad when she could see two waiters hovering at their table with the first course.

Afterwards, Morton asked Jackie to dance, leaving Dick to do so with Robyn. Brad seemed in no mood to leave the table and appeared to be listening intently to the sibilant whispering of his companion.

'Quite an eyeful, isn't she?' Dick commented, moving languidly in time to the music.

'Aren't they all?'

He grinned. 'I wish I could say it's because he's a celebrity! But it's more than that. Even if he were a beach boy he'd attract the stunners. I guess it's the indifferent way he looks at women that makes them all come running.' Brown eyes regarded her. 'All except you, that is. How come?'

'You know the old saying about no man being a hero to his valet? Well, you can also substitute secretary for that.'

Dick laughed. 'I don't believe Brad has any faults that would turn a girl off.'

Robyn refused to be drawn, knowing only too well how show-business—indeed how most people—loved to gossip.

'What did it feel like going back to a humdrum job after being at the villa?' he went on.

Seizing on the opportunity to talk on a subject unconnected with Brad, she told him of her change of status.

'As a matter of fact,' she informed him, 'I've a new author who I think would be excellent at doing TV plays. Her plots are strong and her dialogue is excellent.'

'Have her submit an outline to me and I'll let you know what I think of it.'

'That's what I'd already planned to do. You'll have it on your desk first thing Monday morning.'

'You're a fast worker,' he commented.

'Only in business!'

They were both smiling and relaxed when they returned to the table, though Robyn had no appetite for food and pushed it from one side of her plate to the other. Brad was still giving all his attention to his companion, and as the main course was cleared away, he pulled her to her feet and began to dance, Morton immediately did the same with Robyn.

'Do you know you're the loveliest looking girl in the room?' he said seriously. 'And probably the only natural blonde!'

'The last comment I'll believe,' she smiled.

'You can believe the first one too. In that red dress you look so exotic no one would ever believe you're just a homebody at heart.'

'Shush!' She put a finger to his mouth. 'That's my secret, remember? Don't let anyone hear you.'

'Meaning Brad?'

Before she could answer, he executed two intricate steps which brought them closer to the man of whom he had just been speaking.

'I'm pushing you off the deep end again,' he murmured. 'You can't keep running away.'

One more nifty piece of footwork and they were alongside Brad and the blonde, with Morton suavely insisting they change partners.

With an immense effort of will Robyn did not tense as Brad's arms came around her. His hands were warm upon her waist and she forced herself to think of them as any hands, and not the ones which had caressed her so intimately that they had almost brought her to surrender. With another supreme effort she tilted her head to look at him. Only inches apart, she saw that the lines fanning out from his eyes were more noticeable than when she had seen him six months ago. It gave him a tired look, though it did not detract from his appeal; rather it enhanced it, making her long to gather him close and comfort him. What a laugh that would give him! Hadn't he once told her he detested motherly women?

'Working on a new book?' she asked brightly.

'You sound like Morton.'

'He'll be pleased to hear it. I'm one of his editors now. He thinks I'm rather good.'

'I bet he does!'

There was no mistaking Brad's meaning, and anger trembled through her.

'Don't be obvious, Brad,' she said coldly. 'It doesn't become you.'

'I'm always obvious. Women prefer me that way.'

For answer Robyn let her eyes move to his girl-friend, who was snuggling up to Morton. 'Your newest?' she asked.

'A fill-in. She's flying back to New York the day after tomorrow. I only brought her along to maintain my image. It wouldn't do for me to arrive in England without a lovely in tow.'

'I'm not so sure. The media might find it such a surprise that you'd probably get more publicity out of it.'

'But not as much fun,' he mocked. 'Tina's very inventive.'

Robyn closed her eyes, afraid he would see the pain in them.

'Don't go to sleep on me,' said Brad, giving her a slight shake. 'Though I wouldn't mind you doing it *with* me.'

Her lids lifted sharply. 'You're still not my type.'

'So I remember you telling me. What's happened to your two Scotsmen? Have they drowned themselves in a loch?'

'They're both perfectly well,' she said stiffly.

'Haven't you made up your mind which of them to choose, or do you have somebody new?'

'There's always somebody new,' she said flippantly. 'But I invariably go back to Hamish and Alex. Don't let's talk about me. I'm more interested in hearing about your new book. I know you haven't mentioned anything to Morton and he's dying of curiosity.'

Brad was silent for a moment. 'I've given up non-fiction,' he said finally. 'I'm working on a novel.'

Robyn was so startled that she missed a step and Brad's hand tightened on her.

'Why the surprise?' he drawled.

'I just assumed you'd go on milking your reputation. I'm sure it's good for another three books on the same subject.'

'I'm bored with it.'

'Only the writing of it, though?' Her eyes again moved to the blonde.

'If you're still so curious about my love life, Robyn, why not take up my earlier offer? It still stands, you know. I might even make it a year instead of six months.'

'My old reply stands too,' Robyn replied with commendable coolness. 'Please don't become a bore on the subject.'

She heard his breath catch sharply, but he gave no other sign of anger. The tempo of the music changed and became languorous, and Brad drew her close against his body. He made no effort to dance the way Morton did, but barely moved in time to the music, making it clear he was on the floor because it was the only socially acceptable way of holding a girl in his arms in public. How clearly he indicated that he wanted to do much more than hold!

Robyn tried to draw away from him, but he would not let her, curving his body into hers, the hardening of his muscles making words unnecessary.

'I like your new hairstyle,' he commented huskily. 'Don't ever cut your hair short, Robyn.'

She tried to think of a flippant reply, but none came to mind. All she could think of was the pain and joy of being in Brad's arms, and of the effort she must make not to let him know it. With deepfelt relief she heard a soft roll on the drums, then she and Brad were moving back to the table.

For the rest of the evening he did not look her way. He danced with Jackie and his girl-friend, and then at midnight left them, giving Robyn no more than a cursory glance.

It was nearly an hour later before the rest of the party broke up, and as the doorman went off to get their cars, Dick reminded Robyn to send him the outline of the play she had promised.

'I'll fix up a date with you as soon as I've read it. Can we talk about it over dinner one night?'

'Only if there's something to talk about,' she smiled.

'I'll find something,' he teased.

'Dick can always find something,' Jackie laughed, and gave Robyn a wide smile. 'You can see I lost out with lover-boy,' she added. 'I'm back among the ranks.'

Robyn thought of this comment as she lay sleepless in bed and watched dawn streak the sky. At least she had one consolation with which to comfort herself. Having refused promotion in Brad's legion of lovelies, he could never relegate *her* to the ranks.

CHAPTER TEN

IT was difficult for Robyn to avoid seeing Brad. All his publicity for the forthcoming series had been arranged by Morton, and either she or someone else from the firm was expected to be with him when he was being interviewed. Robyn managed to avoid most of them, though she was obliged to be present at the literary luncheon given in his honour. Since the theme of it was his latest book, as many beautiful girls as possible had been invited, with the current Miss World sitting on his left and the highest paid model in England on his right.

The speech he gave was a very witty one with many quotable comments in it, all of them cynical, as befitted the image he worked so hard to maintain. Except that using the word 'image' implied that this was not the real man, whereas Robyn knew that it was.

It was well into the afternoon before she made her escape from the flower-filled, perfumed atmosphere, leaving Brad surrounded by adoring women and managing to look faintly bored. It was his hard-to-get attitude, she thought cynically, and knew in that instant that she could not bear to see him again, even if her job depended on it.

Realising it very well might, she saw there was only one way out: to work in a field where she would not be called upon to meet him.

She was still debating where to look and whether she was being foolish to leave her present position, when Dick Summers telephoned to say he liked the play outline she had sent him and wanted to discuss it with her over dinner any evening they were mutually free.

'It's not just an excuse to see you,' he added. 'I really think this writer of yours has potential.'

'I'm free on Thursday,' Robyn told him.

'That's fine with me. I'm meeting Brad for a drink at six-thirty, if you'd care to come along?'

'Not particularly. I'm beginning to find him a bore.'

'I won't quote you,' he chuckled.

'I don't care if you do.' She drew a deep breath. 'If you'd like to meet me another night . . .'

Assuring her Thursday was fine, Dick arranged to call for her at eight, and Robyn found herself wondering if Dick could help her find a job in television. Once they had finished talking about her client, she would start to talk about herself.

Her dinner with Dick was far pleasanter than she had anticipated. Away from the holiday atmosphere of the south of France, he was far less flirtatious, and for nearly an hour they talked about the outline she had submitted. He was critical of a great deal of it and she suggested various ways in which alterations and amendments could be done.

'Are these your suggestions, or did your author give you a lead?' he asked.

'They're all mine,' she admitted. 'But they're pretty obvious ones. Miss Bancroft, I know, would have come up with them herself if you'd met her.'

'I wonder. You have an excellent imagination, and you're quick with it. Ever thought of doing any writing yourself?'

'Many times,' she said wryly. 'But I don't have an original mind. Give me something to work on and I'm great at expanding it. But sit me in front of a blank sheet of paper and nothing happens.'

'You'd make a good script editor if you're ever interested in changing your job.'

Here was the opening she wanted, and she grasped it with both hands. Before the evening was out, Dick had offered her the chance of working as script editor with

him on a new series of one-hour plays which he was producing for the coming autumn. It was exactly the sort of
job she knew she would enjoy, yet something held her
back from accepting it. No, not something, she admitted
with honesty, someone. Bradley Dexter. Working with
Dick would still keep her in Brad's world; hearing gossip
about him; knowing what he was doing, and with whom;
probably even having to meet him from time to time. As
these were the three factors that had decided her to leave
Morton, it would be illogical to work for Dick. She
searched for an acceptable way of refusing his offer and
finally decided to get as near to the truth as she could.

'I want to get away from the flip side of life, Dick. I'd
prefer to work on serious documentaries, and the sort of
plays you're planning aren't quite what I had in mind.'

'You don't have the experience to get much of a job on
documentaries,' he warned, clearly disappointed by her
refusal to accept his offer.

'I realise that, but I'm prepared to start at the bottom
and work my way up.'

Intelligent enough to know he would not be able to
make her change her mind, Dick proved himself to be a
good friend by arranging for her to meet Johnson Cabot,
renowned documentary producer and regular winner of
some of the most prestigious awards.

'People are willing to work for Cabot for nothing just
in order to learn from him,' Dick warned, 'but if I recommend you he'll at least see you. The rest is up to you.'

Although she knew the chance of being offered a job by
Johnson Cabot was remote, Robyn felt she owed it to
Morton to tell him she was going to see the man.

'I can't say I'm surprised,' he confessed, regarding her
across his desk. 'You decided to leave here when Brad
came over to promote his new series, didn't you?'

'Yes. I thought I might change my mind once he
returned to the States, but I haven't.' Her eyes moved to

the shelves behind Morton's head—here were the books of the authors he personally favoured, and half of one shelf was given over to the works of Bradley Dexter.

Following the movement of her eyes, Morton frowned. 'You can't run away from your feelings, Robyn. Stand still and fight them.'

'You've told me that before,' she said ruefully, 'but it hasn't worked. I need to be in a completely different environment.'

'And to have another man,' Morton added, and came round the side of the desk to kiss her lightly on the cheek. 'I wish it could have been me, my dear, but since it can't, I think you're doing the wisest thing by leaving.'

She was touched by his concern and smiled tremulously at him. 'Mr Cabot may send me away with a flea in my ear! In which case you'll be stuck with me until I find something else.'

But Mr Cabot did not send her away. He took an instant liking to her and asked her to sit in and take notes on a conference he was conducting that very morning; then asked for her comments on it.

Tentatively she gave them, apologising for her lack of knowledge, yet still having the courage to be critical about some of the points which had been discussed. The man heard her out in silence, frowning occasionally, but when she had finished he gave a brief nod.

'I agree with most of what you've said, Robyn. You've shown a quicker grasp of the situation than many of my own team would have done. Start work on Monday.'

Her pulses leapt with pleasure. 'That's wonderful, Mr Cabot! Thank you. But I'll need to give Mr Phillips a month's notice.'

'Then forget it. If you can't start at once, you're no good to me.'

'If I walked out on *you* without warning, I wouldn't be good for you either,' Robyn said at the door, and was halfway through it when he called her back.

'All right, four weeks, then. But if you can make it less, do so.'

Appreciating her anxiety to start her life afresh, Morton agreed to let Robyn go in a fortnight, and the weekend before she was due to leave him, she visited her parents to tell them of her new plans.

No matter how busy she was, she never allowed anything to interfere with her monthly visit home. Indeed, the more hectic her schedule, the more she enjoyed the relaxation of being with two people with whom she could be completely herself.

'I saw Bradley Dexter on the Saturday chat show,' her mother said when they were all sitting round the fireside after dinner, with Alex on Robyn's lap and Hamish resting his head on her feet, his sturdy little body twitching as he dreamed happy doggy dreams. 'He's an exceptionally good-looking man,' her mother continued.

'Exceptionally.'

'Do you still feel the same way about him?'

Robyn was too startled to hide her surprise and her mother, an older edition of her daughter, though not as slender, gazed back at her unwaveringly.

'How did you know?' Robyn asked slowly.

'Because you've never talked to us about him. Normally you always give us vivid descriptions of the men you meet and make us laugh about their faults.'

'Brad has too many to laugh about.'

'He does have a somewhat wild reputation,' her mother agreed. 'But I wasn't sure if the newspapers were exaggerating.'

'Not in this case. He's exactly the way they describe him. It amazes me that he can stand the strain of the way he lives,' Robyn added waspishly.

'The strain isn't doing *you* any good either. You're even thinner than you were a month ago.'

Mr Barrett, who had been silent until now, came vigorously into the conversation. He was a burly man, in his late sixties, with the same grey eyes as Robyn.

'Your mother's right. If you're still pining for the fellow, maybe you should have a change of scene. Move to a different job, or go abroad for a while.'

Here was Robyn's chance to tell them she was leaving Morton Phillips, and both her parents were delighted, particularly her father, who was a great admirer of Johnson Cabot's work.

'I've read something about this new documentary series of his,' Mr Barrett put in. 'It's about children on the poverty line in Europe.'

'Rather a harrowing subject,' his wife added.

'Just the sort of thing to get Robyn's mind off this fancy fellow of hers,' her father said.

It amused Robyn to hear Brad referred to in this way. He wouldn't like to be called a fancy fellow, yet that was exactly what he was—a man who refused to look below the surface of life and who mocked anyone who did.

At the end of January, Robyn started work for Johnson Cabot and within a month felt she had never done anything else in her life. Although he had engaged her as a junior assistant, he was never too busy to listen to her opinions, or to tell her if he thought them wrong and why. In his late fifties, all the people who worked for him were considerably younger, and he never allowed their youth to be a deterrent in their advancement.

'I had to wait till I was in my late thirties before I was given a chance to show my ability, but these days young people are born mature.'

'And we feel passé at forty,' one of the young men joked.

'One day I'll do a documentary about age versus youth,' the older man said, 'showing that when you reach a certain point in your life, age no longer matters.'

'For men maybe,' Robyn interpolated. 'It always matters to women.'

Johnson Cabot hesitated, then nodded. 'I wish I could disagree with you, my dear, but man—being the creature he is—makes me concede the argument.'

'Age only matters to a woman when it comes to the physical side of her life,' another young girl put in. 'But aren't we discussing the wider aspect?'

'One can never ignore a woman's personal life,' the man said. 'Love has a habit of infiltrating into every area of her existence. In that sense men are luckier. No matter how in love they are, they can always relegate it to the back of their mind and blank it off.'

How true, Robyn thought, as Brad inevitably came into her mind. It was strange how often he still did; as much now as when she had first left France. Sometimes his image was so strong that she despaired of ever forgetting him.

His television series was over. It had been a great success and there was talk of it receiving an Emmy in America, the television equivalent of the film world's Oscar. Yet of Brad himself there was hardly any news. He had apparently left his Bel Air home, but no one knew where he was. However, this did not stop the gossip columnists from hazarding their guesses. Cruising in the Caribbean with the lovely divorcee Dolores del Costa, opined one. Hiding in the Swiss chalet of Baroness von Hoffmeyer, vouchsafed another. On the Australian range of cattleman's daughter Jane Dunlop, asserted a third. But there were never any pictures to substantiate their claims and Robyn had no means of knowing whether they were true. Of one thing only was she certain: wherever he was, there would be a girl with him.

Winter slowly passed. Robyn was promoted and the first two of Johnson Cabot's documentaries were completed. Work went ahead on the third and Robyn found herself with hardly a moment to spare, so that even going to Wiltshire for her monthly visits became difficult. But knowing how much her parents looked forward to them, she always squeezed them in, even if she had to cut the time and go down on Sunday instead of Saturday.

On this particular weekend in March she was doing exactly that and, too tired to face the prospect of driving, decided to travel by train. At least that way she would be able to relax for a few hours.

She reached the station with barely a moment to grab a magazine and rush to her seat, flinging herself into the carriage even as the train began to move. Her magazine and handbag went flying, and a tweedy-dressed man sitting in the corner of the otherwise empty compartment bent to retrieve them.

As he straightened, their eyes met, and both man and girl were taken by surprise.

'Hello, Robyn,' Martin recovered first. 'Long time no see.'

The colour came and went in her face and she sat down shakily. She had not given Martin a thought since she had last seen him in France, when he had accepted Brad's word that she was having an affair with Morton. As she remembered this her manner was distant.

'Are you in England on holiday?' she asked coolly.

'An extended one. For three months, actually. Brad's new book is in manuscript stage and he always likes to work on the final corrections himself.'

'Ah yes, he mentioned that he was writing a book when I last saw him.' She was still cool. 'A novel, I think?'

'One of the best I've read,' Martin informed her. 'An amalgamation of *David Copperfield* and *The Carpetbaggers*!'

'I can't imagine it!'

'Well, it's the story of a man's life from childhood to middle age, and with no holds barred in describing everything.'

'One of *those* sort of books,' Robyn said dismissively.

'Wait till you read it,' Martin reproved, and leaned forward to look at her more closely. 'You're not very friendly, Robyn. What have I done to annoy you?'

'Nothing. But we weren't particularly friendly when we parted.'

He had the grace to redden, but did not look away. 'I accept that I had no right to moralise, but I'd fallen hard for you and I was bitterly upset. I'd imagined you to be different from—from what you were.'

'I haven't changed.' Her voice dripped ice and, abashed by it, he sank back into his seat.

'I don't normally set myself up as a judge of people's morality,' he said after several minutes had passed. 'It was only with you that . . . Oh hell! I guess I'm looking for the impossible.'

Some of Robyn's anger abated. Martin was indeed searching for a rarity these days—as she herself was doing— but it was not an impossible task. Darn it, she wasn't the only girl with old-fashioned notions about physical love and the sanctity of marriage. Any more than he was the only man. Yet she dared not tell him the truth about herself.

'What are you doing on this train?' he broke into her thoughts.

'Visiting my parents. They live in Little Crompton.'

'How strange—I'm visiting friends a few miles from there. I don't suppose you'd . . .'

'No.'

Once more there was silence.

'Where's Brad these days?' she asked casually.

'At the villa.'

'In France? How come no one's found out?'

'Because he's keeping a low profile. No dining out and no entertaining. Just work.'

'And women,' she added sweetly.

'Not one.'

'Safety in numbers?'

'None,' he stated. 'For the past five months, since he came to London for the launch of his television series, he hasn't looked at a girl.'

'Does anyone else know how ill he is?' Robyn asked sarcastically, and Martin shrugged.

'He's a changed man, Robyn. I don't know what's happened to him, but he's not the same man he was.'

'Maybe his hectic life has finally caught up with him.'

'Maybe it has.' Martin's voice was unexpectedly sharp. 'It could happen to you, too.'

'I won't wait till I'm as old as Brad before changing my life-style. As a matter of fact I'm thinking of doing it now,' she fabricated. 'I never thought I'd be willing to give up my freedom for any man, but when love hits you . . .'

Martin looked at her intently. 'So you've finally fallen?'

'Hook, line and sinker.'

He digested this, running a hand through his sandy brown hair. 'Perhaps I should have been more persevering with you.'

'It wouldn't have helped you, I'm afraid. You were no more my type than Brad.'

Instead of being annoyed, he looked contrite, as if realising he deserved the reprimand, and Robyn was ashamed of her loss of temper. After all, why should she blame Martin for her unhappiness? What he thought of her was of little importance. It was Brad whose low opinion of her had hurt her so badly. If only he had loved her enough to ask her to stay with him indefinitely—even without marriage—instead of putting a limit on it; as if his desire for her was something that would wear out within a given time.

'I'll tell Brad I saw you,' Martin murmured as the train

pulled into the small country station.

'Why bother?' she shrugged, and collecting her over-night case, set off down the platform, with Martin striding beside her.

Her father was standing by his Rover and came forward to greet her. Briefly Robyn introduced the two men, then hurriedly steered her father to the car.

'Friend of yours?' he enquired as they drove off.

'Bradley Dexter's secretary.'

'Ah.' There was a significant pause, which Robyn read all too well.

'I'm afraid so,' she admitted at last. 'But it's getting better all the time. This week I hardly thought of him.'

Robyn kept repeating this to herself throughout the weekend, but the unexpected encounter with Martin re-awakened all her memories, making it impossible for her to relax. She managed to hide her restlessness from her parents, but it was a relief to return to London and start work again on Monday.

One day followed another, and she was glad of the increasing pressure of work. This way she had no time to brood on the past or contemplate the lonely future. Indeed she was so absorbed in the present that when she picked up the telephone in her office three weeks later, it took her a moment to recognise Morton Phillips' voice.

'How are things going?' he asked. 'You seem to have dropped out of circulation.'

'I've been busy,' she explained.

'Too busy to have dinner with me?'

Remembering his many kindnesses to her, she was unwilling to say no, and agreed to meet him at the White Tower the following evening.

He was already waiting for her when she arrived, and she was warmed by the sight of him.

'You look good enough to eat,' he said, kissing her on

the cheek and retaining hold of her hand while they sat down.

'Not better than the duck they serve here!' she grinned, pushing her hair away from her face and looking around.

It was a restaurant that was particularly enjoyable to go to in the evening, when the soft lights and faintly Victorian air gave it a *fin de siècle* atmosphere. As usual, the food was excellent and Robyn stuck to the choice she always made when she came here: two pâtés as hors d'oeuvre, followed by crisp roast duck and a fresh fruit salad that was second to none.

It was far more pleasant to be with Morton than she had recollected. She knew him well enough to relax completely with him, and had no need to make conversation.

'If only you were nearer to me in age,' he said, sipping his brandy and eyeing her over the balloon rim.

She smiled but made no comment.

'No regrets at leaving me?' he probed.

'Not enough to make me change my mind and come back.'

'Pity. You had the makings of a first class editor. I don't suppose you'd care to do any reading for me in your spare time?'

'I'd be delighted—if I had any spare time.'

'That's what I thought,' he said regretfully. 'Pity. I've a particular manuscript I'd have liked your opinion on.'

Her curiosity was piqued. 'What sort of manuscript?'

'A novel from a new author. I read it over the weekend and I've had two readers' reports since. But I'd have welcomed yours.'

It was flattering to be asked in this way, and though she knew she was falling for the flattery, Robyn found herself agreeing to read the book.

'Send it to me on Friday and I'll let you have it back by Monday.'

'I can do even better than that,' he replied, and lifted

up a parcel under the table.

'You're incorrigible!' she laughed. 'You knew I'd agree.'

'All I knew was that you have a kind nature and that I'm a big enough swine to take advantage of it!'

Although it was late when Robyn returned home, curiosity compelled her to undo the parcel, and she gave a groan as she saw the fat wadge of typescript. Two hundred thousand words at least. Damn Morton! Slipping the book into a drawer, she knew that her whole weekend would be spent reading it.

On Friday afternoon Johnson Cabot surprised everyone by announcing that his third documentary film was being delayed and that he was going to New York for three months. It was an unpleasant blow for Robyn, for though the television company employing Mr Cabot would pay the wages of all his staff, she knew she would be assigned to a different job. After thinking about it for several hours, she went to Mr Cabot's offfce and told him she would prefer to leave.

'I enjoyed working for *you*,' she stressed, 'but I don't want any old job in television.'

'You're too bright to have to make do with "any old job". Why not wait and see what you're offered before you make any hasty decision?'

Accepting the wisdom of this, Robyn agreed, though the prospect of yet another employer disconcerted her, increasing the restlessness that she thought she had conquered after she had left her job with Morton.

Returning to her flat earlier than usual, she took out the manuscript, deciding now was as good a time as any to begin it. Maybe her dinner with Morton had been fortuitous, for she could do a lot worse than return to her old job. From the praise he had heaped upon her, she could look forward to going back to an even better one. Comforted by this, she curled up on the settee, opened the first page of the typescript and started to read.

From the moment Robyn absorbed the first page, she knew that Morton had discovered a great new talent. By one o'clock that morning, after several hours of reading, she was convinced of it. The prose was crisp, direct, and occasionally lyrical. The story was dramatic and the main character, Hal, a man in the middle years of his life, re-assessing his past in the hope that it would enable him to decide what to do with his future, was one of the most rounded characters she could remember having come across.

It was only when she began to fall asleep over the pages that she reluctantly set the book aside and went to bed. Even then the character of Hal stayed in her thoughts, and in the morning, as soon as she had had breakfast, she returned to the book, reading it solidly until mid-after-noon, when she stopped to make herself a snack.

Although she was only half way through the book she knew it was a tour de force. How cleverly the author kept alive the mystery of the man whose life he was portraying. Even now she could not even guess what the end was going to be. Would Hal forget the misery of his early life and be able to share his future with a woman? Or would the bitterness which had warped him continue to do so until he died?

The choices facing him intrigued her, and she was eager to know which one he finally took. He had too strong an ego to be swayed by emotion alone. Love might give him pause for thought, but it would never give him the vision to see himself as he really was. In that sense he was like Brad, who had wanted her so much that he had asked her to live with him, though he had still been too blinded by his past to admit the depth of his need for her.

She picked up the book to resume reading and then stopped. It was not only Hal and Brad who were blind. She was too. Blind and incredibly stupid. How had it taken her so long to realise that Hal was Brad? *He* was the 'unknown author'. In telling the story of this wealthy man at the crossroads of his life, Brad was looking ahead to the crossroads which he himself would be facing ten years from now, when casual liaisons were no longer satisfying, even temporarily. Given artistic licence, and the changing of certain facts in order to disguise them, most of what she had so far read was identical with the story Brad had told her of his own past.

Pushing the book aside, she dialled Morton's home. Almost as if he had been expecting her call, he answered it immediately.

'Unknown writer be damned!' she flared. 'It's Brad, isn't it? Why couldn't you have been honest and told me?'

'Because I wanted your unbiased opinion. What do you think of it?'

'It's wonderful. What else could I think of it? But you'd no right to do this to me, Morton. It was deceitful of you!'

'I did it for the best,' he apologised. 'You wouldn't have read it if I'd told you he'd written it.'

'I'm not going to read it now,' she stormed. 'Anyway, you don't need my opinion. You know damn well the book's a winner.'

'At least finish it,' he pleaded, not denying her comment. 'Where are you up to?'

'Half way through, and I don't need to read any more.'

'Aren't you curious to know what Hal does with his life?'

'No!'

She banged down the telephone and glared balefully at the manuscript, knowing full well that no matter how hard she tried not to do so, she would eventually pick it up and read it to its conclusion.

Yet she managed to hold out for the remainder of that day and evening, and it was not until Sunday morning, in the middle of trying to concentrate on a particularly boring colour supplement, that she reached for the book again.

By the time she came to the end of the story, she was making no attempt to fight back her tears. It was an unexpected finale, yet—logically—the only one possible. Hal had taken none of the decisions open to him and there was no happy end. At fifty he was too old to give up his hatred of his past, and not young enough to make anything of the future that was left to him. Bitterness had been the rudder that had steered his ship, and he was clever enough to realise that if he cut it loose, he might founder. Already it was obvious to the reader that he would become even richer, yet grow poorer in spirit with each passing year. The anguish of the final paragraph etched itself in Robyn's mind, for it was here that Hal faced his empty soul, seeing the image of himself which he'd worshipped for too long, and which had set too solid for him to break.

The book slipped from her hands and slid to the floor. How much of Hal's thoughts were Brad's, and did he also think he had left things too late? But if he did, why had he written this book? Surely this was his way of extricating himself from his memories? He couldn't have relived all those painful experiences unless he believed it would free him to live and love as he wanted.

Yet Hal was not free.

Robyn drew a shuddering breath, unwilling to think of Brad going on in the same empty way: each year becoming richer in money and poorer in life. The telephone rang and she was as startled as if it were an intruder. She picked it up and heard Morton's voice.

'Don't put the phone down on me,' he said quickly. 'What I have to say is important.'

'I won't put the phone down,' she said quietly. 'I've just finished the book.'

'I'm glad.' he hesitated. 'That makes it easier for me to say what I have to.'

'What is it, Morton?' She was disturbed by his tone. 'Is anything wrong?'

'No, but . . . well, Brad's in town. He arrived an hour ago and came to see me straight away. He wants your address. He tried looking it up, but you're ex-directory, so he called to see me.'

'You didn't give it to him?' Robyn jumped to her feet—almost as if she expected Brad to burst in on her.

'Of course I didn't,' Morton assured her. 'I wanted to check with you first.'

'Well, don't tell him. I don't want him to have it. We've nothing to say to each other.'

'Obviously Brad doesn't agree, or he wouldn't be trying to contact you. To be honest, my dear, I can't see why you shouldn't meet him. I mean, you've read his new book. Surely that tells you something?'

'Only that he's an excellent writer. But I knew that already.'

'Don't play dumb, girl! That manuscript is more than just a book. It's a testament to the way Brad's changed.'

'I'm not convinced.'

'You might be if you saw him. If you'd heard the way he pleaded with me to give him your address, you wouldn't be so damned stubborn!'

'I'm not being stubborn, Morton. I'm being realistic. I knocked Brad's ego when I turned him down, and he can't forget it.'

'He can't forget *something*,' Morton agreed, 'but it's more than ego. I've never seen him in such a state. He's lost weight and his face is haggard.'

'Overwork,' Robyn retorted. 'I know that from Martin. He hasn't been seeing his friends—or girl-friends either—so maybe he's suffering from withdrawal symptoms! I'm sure the next Miss World will help him recover.'

'You're a hard girl to convince,' Morton muttered.

'Then give up on it and leave me alone. Brad wants me because I said no to him. It's no more than that. If I agreed to live with him, our affair would have been over in six months. Or maybe a year,' she added, remembering his last offer to her. 'And then where would I be?'

'I don't know. But perhaps your assessment of the situation is wrong. Maybe he's changed his mind.'

'No. And you must give me your word that you won't tell him where I live.'

'You already have my word.'

With Morton's call over, Robyn knew she could not remain in the flat. Though she trusted him not to tell Brad where she was, it would not take him long to find out for himself. Dick Summers knew her address, and so might one or two other people at the television company. It was this fear that decided her to go down to Wiltshire. She had no job at the moment and she could do with a break.

Putting her thoughts into action, she speedily packed, left a note for the milkman, and took a taxi to the station. She had two hours to wait for a train, but felt safer in the anonymity of a waiting room rather than in her living room; at least Brad would never think to look for her here.

The Sunday train journey was a tedious one, and she was tired and cold by the time she finally arrived at her parents' house. Seeing the lights gleaming in the darkness, and walking up the small curving drive towards the front door, she felt as if she were returning to the comfort of the womb. It was only a temporary comfort, for she could not shut herself away from the world indefinitely. But by dropping out of circulation she hoped she was finally making it clear to Brad that she did not want to be part of his life.

Although her parents were surprised to see her, they

did not question her unexpected arrival, nor her announcement that she intended to stay with them for several days.

For the first two, she was on tenterhooks, jumping every time the telephone rang and glancing fearfully out of the window each time a car approached. But on the fourth day Morton telephoned to say Brad was leaving for France.

'When I didn't get a reply from your flat, I guessed you were at your parents',' he added. 'I thought you'd like to know it's safe to come out of hiding.'

'I wasn't hiding,' she lied. 'Nor am I coming back to London just yet.'

'When you do return, I hope it'll be to work for me?'

'Don't bank on it,' she warned. 'I may go abroad for six months.'

His sigh came down the receiver. 'It's your life, Robyn. If you're happy to keep running away . . .'

'Goodbye, Morton,' she said crossly. 'I'll be in touch.'

Later that day, ashamed of her irritability towards a man who had always been kind to her, she dropped him a short note of apology, and went out to post it, taking Hamish and Alex with her. The two Scotties barked deliriously as they trotted with her down the drive. Each time she looked at them she was reminded of the ridiculous story she had spun to Brad about them, but short of asking her mother to change their names, there was nothing she could do to forget it.

It was a blustery day and she walked briskly. Hamish could manage it, but Alex began to slow down as she reached the village, and she picked him up and tucked him under her arm. She set him down again as she reached the post office, then turned to make sure Hamish had come in with her too. From the corner of her eye she glimpsed the flash of a low-slung red car, and spun fully round to look at it. Brad's Ferrari. It was too much of a coincidence for it to belong to anyone else.

Stepping back out of sight, but still able to watch, she saw the car slow down and draw to a stop. She glimpsed Brad's face as he leaned out of the window and spoke to an elderly passerby. The woman turned and pointed up the hill, and Robyn realised Brad was asking directions to her home. Thank heavens she was out! Rummaging in her bag for a coin, she went to the telephone box and called her mother.

'Bradley Dexter's on his way to see you,' she said breathlessly. 'He'll be with you in about five minutes. Whatever you do, don't tell him I'm staying with you.'

'What else should I tell him?' her mother expostulated. 'He must know you're not in London if he's coming here.'

'Tell him I only came down for a day and then went to——'

'I've no intention of lying to the man,' her mother interrupted. 'You can behave to him the way you like— that's your prerogative—but if he asks *me* where you are, I'll say you've gone for a walk. If you want to skulk away and hide until he's left, then do so!'

The receiver went down at the other end and Robyn heard the dialling tone.

Surprised by her mother's unexpected attitude, she posted her letter to Morton and slowly went from one shop in the village to another: buying a packet of envelopes she did not want and a lipstick that was the wrong colour. Gradually she came to the realisation that her mother was right. She had been behaving foolishly and childishly. By not seeing Brad she was encouraging him to come after her. She should face him and make it clear that she had no interest in him.

Whistling the dogs to heel, she set off for home. Her steps slowed as she reached the lane leading to the house, and faltered noticeably as she turned into the driveway.

But Brad's car was not there, and she ran the last few yards.

Her parents were alone in the drawing room and she looked from one to the other.

'What happened? Didn't he come?'

'Yes, dear,' her mother said. 'But he only stayed a short while.'

Hamish and Alex flopped in front of the fire, both panting, and Robyn settled herself on the rug beside them.

'What did you think of him?' she asked slowly.

'Don't ask me,' said her father. 'I barely spoke more than a dozen words to him.'

'Your father was in the library when Mr Dexter first arrived,' her mother explained. 'I told him you were out and that I wasn't sure when you'd be back, so he asked if he could wait.' Her mother paused. 'He's even more handsome in real life than he is in his photographs or on television. And so unassuming too. But very nervous.'

'Brad's never nervous.'

'He was—extremely so. He kept wandering round the room, blurting things out to me as if he couldn't help himself.'

Robyn frowned. This did not seem like the Bradley Dexter she knew. 'What sort of things?'

'About the mess he'd made of his life in the past nine months, and how he hoped he hadn't left things too late. He rather took it for granted that I knew what he was talking about,' her mother went on apologetically, 'so I didn't question him. Then your father came in and asked where you were, and I said you'd gone out with Hamish and Alex. That seemed to upset Mr Dexter even more and he became extremely agitated and asked me if I approved of it.'

Robyn jerked upright. 'What did you say to that?' she asked in a strangled voice.

'I didn't quite know what to say,' her mother admitted. 'I mean, his behaviour was so extraordinary. He was fairly

pale when he arrived, but the moment he heard me mention Hamish and Alex he went absolutely ashen. I told
him I thoroughly approved of your going out with them—
much better than having you indoors moping—and before
I could say another word, he announced that he wasn't
going to wait for you after all.'

Robyn swallowed hard. She did not know whether to
laugh or cry, but neither emotion seemed appropriate.

'I do wish you'd tell us what's going on,' her father said
into the silence. 'I realise we're only your parents,
but . . .'

'Brad believes that Hamish and Alex are two important
men in my life,' she said boldly. 'He doesn't realise they're
dogs.'

Her mother and father looked at her blankly, then
began to smile. Robyn smiled too, even though tears were
still near.

'Do you think you could tell us how the misunder-
standing arose?' her mother suggested. 'I'm sure you had
a good reason for letting Mr Dexter believe such an
extraordinary thing.'

'A very good reason,' Robyn agreed, and with a little
monitoring, recounted the story of her arrival and stay at
the villa.

'The truth would have been a far better weapon than
two dogs,' Mr Barrett snorted at the end of the saga. 'If
he hadn't wanted a young innocent working for him, he
could have sent you packing.'

'That's what I was afraid he'd do,' Robyn explained.
'And I didn't want him to. You see, I had to get him to
finish that book for Morton.'

'Why didn't you tell him the truth afterwards?' her
mother asked.

'What would have happened then? You're not saying I
should have agreed to his proposition and lived with
him?'

'No, dear, I'm not. But at least once you'd left him, he'd have been able to re-assess the position—based upon the truth—whereas at the moment he's judging you from a totally false premise.'

'If he'd known the real you,' Mr Barrett intervened, 'he might not have suggested you live with him in the first place. But you yourself gave the impression you were set against marriage, so that even if he'd wanted it, he'd have been nervous of asking you. In my opinion, you should tell him the truth about yourself.'

Robyn tried not to be swayed by her parents, but it was a losing battle. Anyway, they were right; had she not been afraid of Brad hurting her, she would have realised it for herself. She should have been honest with him when she had seen him in London in January. Instead of which she had allowed her jealousy of Miss *Playboy* Centrefold to force her into continuing her charade. True, the net result for Brad had been a reassessment of himself and the writing of an excellent novel, but what he would do from here on, she could not even begin to guess. But she knew what she had to do.

'I'm going to see him and tell him the truth,' she said aloud.

'He's staying at the Connaught,' her mother vouchsafed.

'I won't call him. This is something I must say to his face.'

Because there were no further trains to London, Robyn borrowed her mother's car, pushing the little Volvo flat out. Even so it was well after eight before she stepped into the Connaught lobby and asked the reception clerk to tell Mr Dexter she was downstairs.

'I'm afraid Mr Dexter checked out an hour ago,' he said. 'He was catching the night ferry to Calais.'

This was something Robyn had not expected. For an instant she did not know what to do, then she realised there was only one possible solution.

Returning to her flat, she telephoned her parents and then packed her suitcase. It was only as she checked her passport that she realised she might arrive at the villa to discover Brad had remained in Paris. After all, why shouldn't he? Believing she was still with Hamish and Alex, he would see no reason to go on hoping they had a future together. The thought of what he might do set her afire with jealousy, and she wished wholeheartedly she had rushed out to the car when she had seen him through the post office window. But since it was impossible to undo the past, her only hope lay in unravelling the future. Determinedly she dialled the villa.

The telephone rang for some time and she was in the act of replacing it when she heard Kim's voice. After a brief greeting, she came to the point.

'I want to see Mr Dexter, Kim, but I don't want to come down unless I'm sure he'll be there.'

'He arriving day after tomorrow,' Kim assured her. 'He phone from hotel before he leave London.'

'Then I'll arrive the day after tomorrow too. But please don't tell him. I want it to be a surprise.'

With a day to kill, Robyn took herself round the shops. Never had the time hung so heavy, and she whiled it away buying presents for Kim and his wife, some clothes for herself and a special present for Brad.

'Your little boy will love these,' said the shop assistant in Harrods, wrapping them up.

'They're for a big boy,' said Robyn, straight-faced, 'and he may well hate them!'

She thought of this again when, at two-thirty the next day, she walked out into the spring sunshine at Nice airport. It was hard to believe it was nine months since she had been here. Her memory of that time was so vivid it seemed as if it were yesterday. Yet the anguish she had endured since leaving here had frequently made her feel that each moment had been stretched into infinity.

The villa looked exactly as she remembered it: the grass greener perhaps and the bougainvillaea not yet out, though a blaze of golden mimosa lit up the long drive. The garage doors were wide open and she glimpsed the Ferrari, before she went round the side of the house to the kitchen.

Mrs Kim was seated at the table cleaning vegetables while her husband polished silver in the butler's pantry. Robyn was touched by their warm welcome, though too anxious to see Brad to spend more than a few minutes with them.

'Mr Dexter on terrace,' said Kim. 'You go see him and I take cases to old room.'

'I'd like to go up and change first,' she said quickly, and put her finger to her lips to warn him to keep her arrival quiet.

Smiling conspiratorially, he ushered her up the servants' staircase to the first floor. She felt a sense of homecoming when she entered the bedroom she had previously occupied, and unpacked quickly before slipping into a fuchsia sun-dress. The present she had bought Brad lay at the bottom of her case and she took it out and undid it. Where should she leave it? There was only one answer, and she hurried up the spiral staircase to his bedroom and placed the two objects on his pillow.

Then it was downstairs again, rubber-soled sandals noiseless on the marble floor. Entering the living room she was again struck by the beautiful view. The sky was the colour of spring bluebells, the almond trees green as fresh lettuce and the distant palms on the lower lawn swayed their heads in the gentle breeze. Her eyes searched the terrace for Brad and found him sitting in an armchair, profile towards her.

Whatever his thoughts, they were not happy ones, for there was an unutterably sad expression on his face. This was the Bradley Dexter no outsider was ever permitted to see, and guiltily Robyn knew she shouldn't be seeing it either; not yet, at least; not until the situation had been resolved between them. She no longer questioned how long she would be staying here. She was here and that was all that mattered. His behaviour in the last five months—when he'd written his novel—clearly showed that he needed her as much as he wanted her, and if she couldn't use these two emotions to build a future for them both, it would not be for want of trying. Drawing a deep breath, she walked on to the terrace.

'Hullo, Brad.'

He looked around. He gave a slight shake of his head as if uncertain she were real, then slowly stood up.

'You're the last person I expected to see here.' There was no expression in his voice nor on his face.

'I'm sorry I missed you when you came down to Wiltshire,' she continued. 'You should have waited for me.'

'I know, and I was coming back.'

'You were?'

'Yes.' He saw her puzzled look. 'I was just sitting here trying to make up my mind whether I should drive to London today or fly back tomorrow.'

He came a step towards her. Close to, Robyn saw the tiredness in his eyes. It had been there when she had seen him in January and she had accused him of living it up. Now she was beginning to suspect she had misjudged him; that bone-weary look came from a different kind of sleeplessness.

'I shouldn't have walked out of your parents' home the way I did,' he went on. His voice was low and the words ran into each other as if he wanted to get them quickly said. 'I'm everything you've ever accused me of, Robyn— a womaniser, a lecher, a selfish immature swine who's taken nine months of his life to realise it and to change.

Except that I haven't changed as much as I'd hoped,' he confessed wryly. 'I'm still selfish enough to want you on my own terms.'

Her spirits sank, but she did not show it.

'That's why I went berserk when your mother told me you were still seeing Hamish and Alex,' he continued. 'Though perhaps the word jealous is more appropriate.'

'Jealous?'

'Yes. Overwhelmingly, insanely jealous of any man you even smile at, let alone sleep with! That's a turn-up for the book, isn't it? Me—the great believer in sexual freedom—is so damn jealous of you, that I don't want anyone else to even touch your hand!'

'That *is* a turn-up for the book,' she agreed. 'You've never advocated faithfulness before.'

'Because I've never been in love before.' He put out a hand towards her, then dropped it to his side. 'I love you, Robyn. I've never said that to any woman; never believed I ever would. What I feel for you has turned my whole life upside down—made a mockery of all my beliefs and caused me to re-think my entire future.'

'Can love do that?' she asked seriously. 'You're making it sound like a magic word; as if it's capable of making you believe things you've always decried.'

'That's exactly what it's done. Love is magic, Robyn, that's why I tried not to fall under its spell.'

'Then try harder, Brad. It would be a pity to give up all your beliefs for the sake of a temporary affair.' She gave him a wide smile and heard the breath catch in his throat.

'I don't care how temporary you want it to be,' he exclaimed. 'I'll take you on any terms.'

'Isn't that what the girls have usually said to *you*?'

He looked at her blankly; as if the past was so dead for him that not even his memory of it was alive.

'I deserved that,' he said finally, each word heavy with pain.

'Does that mean you're willing to take me on *my* terms, Brad? That I'm free to leave you when I like; free to go with other men?'

He swallowed visibly and half turned away from her. 'I can't chain you to my side, Robyn, though it's what I'd like to do. But of course you're free.'

'Good. That's settled, then,' she said brightly.

'Not quite.' He faced her again. 'I'd better warn you I'll do my best to change your mind. I don't believe you're as hardboiled and free-thinking as you pretend. I think you're afraid of emotion—the way I was. To begin with I thought it had something to do with your background and your parents—the way it did with me—but having met them I realise it must be something else that soured you. But I'll find out what it is and make you sweet again. I'll——'

'Oh, Brad,' she laughed, 'you're talking like a romance writer!'

'I think like one when you're near me. As I've just said, I'll take you for as long as you're willing to stay, but I'm going to do everything in my power to make it permanent.' He put his hands on either side of her waist and drew her closer. 'I'll never want you to go, Robyn.'

'Never is a long time.'

'Not long enough for the brief span of our lives,' he said huskily, and rested his cheek on hers. 'Why did you come to me today? Did you know how empty I felt—how hopeless?'

She longed to say yes, but an imp of mischief, as well as the residue of her own pain, kept her pretending.

'I suddenly realised you were much more my type than Hamish and Alex.'

With a groan he began to kiss her; soft, tender kisses all over her face before he came to her lips. Only then did passion appear, and his arms tightened their hold. Robyn's mouth parted beneath his and she trembled as his hands caressed her body. Yet there was a hesitancy in him and it told her—as clearly as his words—that he was a man afraid; made uncertain by love; weakened by his need of another person and by his fearful recognition of what that need had done to him.

She pushed him gently away, though she still stayed in the circle of his arms. 'Morton sent me your new manuscript, Brad. I'd just finished reading it when he called to tell me you were in London looking for me.'

'Is that why you ran away?' Brad moved back slightly too, his eyes narrowed. 'Didn't you understand what that book meant to me?'

'I wasn't sure.'

'I'm no Hal,' he said forcefully. 'I don't intend spending the rest of my life alone, the way he was going to do. That's why I came in search of you. Why I'll never let you go again.' He cupped her face in his hands. 'One day you might even consider marrying me.'

'I wouldn't look that far ahead,' she murmured, hiding her joy.

'I'm banking on it,' he said firmly. 'And if I can't change your mind, maybe our firstborn will.'

'My, my,' she mocked. 'Children and nappies, is it? You *have* changed!'

'Not in every respect.'

Before she could guess his intention, he swung her up in his arms and headed for the stairs.

Only when they were in his bedroom did he set her on her feet again and begin to undo the buttons of her sundress. Even then his movements were uncertain, as if he were a lover for the first time. As he was, Robyn thought exultantly, for she was the first woman to get under his guard. Tenderly she smoothed her fingers down the column of his neck and over the supple skin on his shoulders. In shorts and tee-shirt he looked like the Brad she had first met, but she knew he was totally different.

Her dress slipped to the floor and she kicked it away with her foot. He looked at her standing supple before him, barely covered by two wisps of underwear. His eyes darkened with desire and he drew her down to the bed. Only then did he see the two little Scotties—one black, one white—on his pillow.

'What on earth . . .?' He reached out for them. They were exquisitely made, with black button eyes and crinkly fur bodies. One wore a blue collar and one a red, each with their name tags on. Brad read them, then raised a perplexed face to hers. 'What are you trying to tell me?'

Demurely she rested her head on a half raised arm. 'Have a guess.'

He bit his lip, still frowning. 'Hamish and Alex,' he read the names aloud. 'You mean they . . . they were never men?'

'Well,' she said hesitantly, keeping a straight face, 'Alex sired Hamish and Hamish has just sired Dougal, so I'd say they were definitely male.'

Brad shook his head like a man in a daze, and changing expressions flitted across his face: incredulity, dismay, anger—definitely anger—and then all at once humour. His mouth curved and he smiled. Then the smile widened and he started to laugh: deep belly laughs that had him flinging himself back against his pillow. But not for long. Abruptly he sat up and leaned towards her, their bodies almost touching.

'Was it all a lie, Robyn? Everything you told me?'

'I'm afraid so. Far from being your idol I detested you and disagreed with everything you advocated in your books. When Morton told me I had to come here I was absolutely furious. And scared, too. I knew that if you tried to seduce me I'd walk out—which would mean Morton not getting the book in time—and I was wondering how I could keep you at arm's length when you suggested I took a nude swim in your pool. That immediately gave me the idea how I should act.'

His mouth curled in reminiscence. 'I remember you made some hardboiled crack when I suggested it.'

'It was all spur-of-the moment stuff,' she admitted. 'Though to be honest, when I came into your room to wake you up on my first morning here, and you jumped out of bed in your birthday suit, I nearly died of fright.'

'So scared?' he teased, his lips nibbling her cheek.

'Petrified.'

'Like now?' he questioned, slipping off his shirt.

'Not quite so petrified.' She pulled his head down and smoothed the black hair away from his forehead. 'That's why I fought you so hard. I knew that once I let you make love to me you'd know what I was really like.' Her voice was a soft thread of sound. 'You'll be the first man, Brad.'

'And the last,' he answered thickly. 'Darling Robyn. Please say I'll be the last.'

'Don't you know without my having to tell you?'

She snuggled closer, burrowing under him. But he resisted and levered himself up from her, placing his hands either side of him.

'There's one question I have to ask you first,' he said quietly. 'If I take you now, will you promise that as soon as I can arrange it, you'll marry me?'

'That's a question I thought you'd never ask!' she cried, winding her arms around him. 'Yes, Brad. Definitely yes!'

The Mills & Boon Rose is the Rose of Romance

Every month there are ten new titles to choose from — ten new
stories about people falling in love, people you want to read
about, people in exciting, far-away places. Choose Mills & Boon.
It's your way of relaxing:

August's titles are:

COLLISION by *Margaret Pargeter*
After the heartless way Max Heger had treated her, Selena wanted
to be revenged on him. But things didn't work out as she had
planned.

DARK REMEMBRANCE by *Daphne Clair*
Could Raina marry Logan Thorne a year after her husband Perry's
death, when she knew that Perry would always come first with her?

AN APPLE FROM EVE by *Betty Neels*
Doctor Tane van Diederijk and his fiancée were always cropping
up in Euphemia's life. If only she could see the back of both of
them?

COPPER LAKE by *Kay Thorpe*
Everything was conspiring to get Toni engaged to Sean. But she
was in love with his brother Rafe — who had the worst possible
opinion of her!

INVISIBLE WIFE by *Jane Arbor*
Vicente Massimo blamed Tania for his brother's death. So how
was it that Tania soon found herself blackmailed into marrying him?

BACHELOR'S WIFE by *Jessica Steele*
Penny's marriage to Nash Devereux had been a ' paper ' one. So
why did Nash want a reconciliation just when Penny wanted to
marry Trevor?

CASTLE IN SPAIN by *Margaret Rome*
Did Birdie love the lordly Vulcan, Conde de la Conquista de Retz
— who wanted to marry her — or did she fear him?

KING OF CULLA by *Sally Wentworth*
After the death of her sister, Marnie wanted to be left alone.
But the forceful Ewan McNeill didn't seem to get the message!

ALWAYS THE BOSS by *Victoria Gordon*
The formidable Conan Garth was wrong in every opinion he held
of Dinah — but could she ever make him see it?

CONFIRMED BACHELOR by *Roberta Leigh*
Bradley Dexter was everything Robyn disliked. But now that she
could give him a well-deserved lesson, fate was playing tricks on
her!